SURVIVORS

THE EMPTY CITY

BY ERIN HUNTER

Willow
Tree

A CIP catalogue record for this book is
available from the British Library

This edition published by Willow Tree Books, 2018
Willow Tree Books, Tide Mill Way, Woodbridge, Suffolk, IP12 1AP
First published in the USA by Harper, an imprint of
Harper Collins Publishers

0 2 4 6 8 9 7 5 3 1

Series created by Working Partners Limited
Copyright © Working Partners 2018
All rights reserved.
Cover illustration © Willow Tree Books 2018
Typography © Willow Tree Books 2018
Endpaper art © Pumbastyle/shutterstock.com 2018

Special thanks to Gillian Philip

Willow Tree Books and associated logos are trademarks and/or
registered trademarks of Imagine That Group Ltd

ISBN: 978-1-78700-444-3
Printed and bound in Great Britain
by Bell and Bain Ltd, Glasgow

www.willowtreebooks.net

With special thanks to Gillian Philip
For Lucy Philip

MEET THE SURVIVORS ...

LONE DOGS

LUCKY – gold-and-white thick-furred male

OLD HUNTER – big and stocky male with a blunt muzzle

LEASHED DOGS

BELLA – gold-and-white thick-furred female, Lucky's littermate (Sheltie-Retriever mix)

DAISY – small white female with a brown tail (Westie/Jack Russell mix)

MICKEY – sleek black-and-white Farm Dog (Border Collie)

MARTHA – giant thick-furred black female with a broad head (Newfoundland)

BRUNO – large thick-furred brown male Fight Dog with a hard face (Bulldog)

SUNSHINE – small female with long white fur (Maltese)

ALFIE – small and stocky blunt-faced dog with mottled brown-and-white fur

WILD DOGS

SWEET – a lean female Greyhound with a long narrow face and smooth, tan-grey fur

FIERCE DOGS

BLADE – large, sleek and muscular female leader of the Fierce Dogs (Doberman)

MACE AND DANGER – muscular bodies, pricked ears and sharp teeth (Dobermans)

PROLOGUE

Yap wriggled, yawning, and gave a small excited whimper. His littermates were a jumble of warmth against him, all paws and muzzles and small fast heartbeats. Clambering over him, Squeak stuck a paw in his eye; Yap shook his head and rolled over, making her fall off. She squeaked with indignation as always, so he licked her nose to show there were no hard feelings.

The Mother-Dog stood over them, nuzzling them into order and licking their faces clean, treading her ritual circle before curling around them, ready for sleep.

"Wake up, Yap! Mother's going to tell us a story." That was Squeak again, bossy and demanding as ever. Their Mother-Dog washed her affectionately with her tongue, muffling her yelps.

"Would you like to hear about the Storm of Dogs?"

A thrill of excitement ran down Yap's spine, and he whimpered eagerly. "Yes!"

"Again?" whined Squeak.

But the others tumbled over her, drowning her protests. "Yes, Mother! The Storm of Dogs!"

The Mother-Dog settled around their small bodies, her tail thumping. Her voice grew low and solemn. "This is the story of Lightning, the swiftest of the dog warriors. The Sky-Dogs watched over him, and protected him … but the Earth-Dog was jealous of Lightning. She thought Lightning had lived too long, and that it was time for him to die so that she could take his life force. But Lightning's speed was so great that he could outrun the Earth-Dog's terrible Growls – he could outrun death itself!"

"I want to be like Lightning," murmured Yowl sleepily. "I could run that fast, I bet I could."

"Shush!" said Squeak, squashing his nose with a golden-furred paw. In spite of her protest, Yap knew that she was caught up in the story like the rest of them.

"Then came the first great battle," the Mother-Dog went on, her voice hushed. "The terrible Storm of Dogs, when all the dogs of the world fought to see who would rule over the territories of the world. Many stories are told of those terrible days, and many heroes were made and lost in the battle.

At last, the Earth-Dog thought, Lightning's life-force would be freed and she would take his body, as was her right. But Lightning was cunning, and he was sure that with his speed he could dodge his death once more, so the Earth-Dog laid a trap for him."

Yip's ears flattened against her head. "That's so mean!"

Their mother nuzzled her. "No, it isn't, Yip. The Earth-Dog was right to claim Lightning. That's the way things should be. When your Sire-Dog died, his body fed the earth too."

Suddenly solemn, all of the pups listened in silence.

"Lightning tried to escape the Storm of Dogs with his speed. He ran so fast between the warring dogs that none of them could see him to tear his body apart with their teeth and claws. He was almost clear, almost free, when the Earth-Dog sent a Big Growl to open the ground in front of him."

Even though he'd heard the story so many times, Yap held his breath and huddled close to his littermates, imagining that this time Lightning would fall and be eaten by the terrible rip in the earth ...

"Lightning saw the ground open up to swallow him,

but he was speeding so fast that he couldn't stop. He feared that the Earth-Dog had him at last. But the Sky-Dogs loved Lightning.

"Just as Lightning started to plummet to his death, the Sky-Dogs sent a great wind that spun so fast and so strong, it caught Lightning as he fell, lifted him up, and whirled him into the sky. And there he remains, with the Sky-Dogs, to this very day."

The pups snuggled more tightly against the Mother-Dog's side, gazing up at her.

"Will he always be there?" asked Yowl.

"Always. When the Sky-Dogs howl and you see fire flashing in the sky, that's Lightning running down to the earth, teasing Earth-Dog, knowing that she will never catch him." She licked Yap's sleepy face. He could barely keep his eyes open. "I've heard dogs say that one day, a dog will displease the Earth-Dog and there will be another great battle. Then, dog will fight against dog, and great heroes will rise and fall. The Storm of Dogs will come again."

Yowl gave a great yawn, floppy with tiredness. "But not for a long time, right?"

"Ah, we don't know. It might come soon; it might not. We must always watch out for the signs. They say that when the world is turned upside down and broken open, the Storm of Dogs will come and we'll have to fight to survive once again."

Yap let his eyelids droop. He loved to fall asleep to his mother's stories. This was how it would always be, he knew: her voice, fading as sleep overwhelmed him and his littermates. The Mother-Dog curled protectively around him; the last thing he heard was the end of the story. It ended the same way each time …

"Watch out, little ones. Watch out for the Storm of Dogs …"

CHAPTER ONE

Lucky startled awake, fear prickling in his bones and fur. He leapt to his feet, growling.

For an instant he'd thought he was tiny once more, safe in his Pup-Pack and protected, but the comforting dream had already vanished. The air shivered with menace, tingling Lucky's skin. If only he could see what was coming, he could face it down – but the monster was invisible, scentless. He whined in terror. This was no sleep-time story: this fear was real.

The urge to run was almost unbearable; but he could only scrabble, snarl and scratch in panic. There was nowhere to go: the wire of his cage hemmed him in on every side. His muzzle hurt when he tried to shove it through the gaps; when he backed away, snarling, the same wire bit into his haunches.

Others were close … familiar bodies, familiar scents. The other dogs were enclosed in this terrible place just as he was. Lucky raised his head and barked, over and over, high and desperate, but it was clear no dog could help him. His voice was drowned out by the chorus of frantic calls.

They were all *trapped.*

Dark panic overwhelmed him. His claws scrabbled at the earth floor, even though he knew it was hopeless.

He could smell the female Swift Dog in the next cage, a friendly, comforting scent, overlaid now with the bitter tang of danger and fear. Yipping, he pressed closer to her, feeling the shivers in her muscles – but the wire still separated them.

"Sweet? Sweet, something's on its way. Something bad!"

"Yes, I feel it! What's happening?"

The longpaws – where were they? The longpaws held them captive in this Trap House, but they had always seemed to care about the dogs. They brought food and water, they laid bedding, cleared the mess …

Surely the longpaws would come for them now.

The others barked and howled as one, and Lucky

raised his voice with theirs.

Longpaws! Longpaws, it's COMING …

Something shifted beneath him, making his cage tremble. In a sudden, terrible silence, Lucky crouched, frozen with horror.

Then, around and above him, chaos erupted.

The unseen monster was here … and its paws were right on the Trap House.

Lucky was flung back against the wire as the world heaved and tilted. For agonizing moments he didn't know which way was up or down. The monster tumbled him around, deafening him with the racket of falling rock and shattering clear-stone. His vision went dark as clouds of filth blinded him. The screaming, yelping howls of terrified dogs seemed to fill his skull. A great chunk of wall crashed off the wire in front of his nose, and Lucky leapt back. Was it the Earth-Dog, trying to take him?

Then, just as suddenly as the monster had come, it disappeared. One more wall crashed down in a cloud of choking dust. Torn wire screeched as a high cage toppled, then plummeted to the earth.

Then there was only silence and a dank metal scent.

Blood! thought Lucky. *Death …*

Panic stirred inside his belly again. He was lying on his side, the wire cage crumpled against him, and he thrashed his strong legs, trying to right himself. The cage rattled and rocked, but he couldn't get up. *No!* he thought. *I'm trapped!*

"Lucky! Lucky, are you all right?"

"Sweet? Where are you?"

Her long face pushed at his through the mangled wire. "My cage door – it broke when it fell! I thought I was dead. Lucky, I'm free – but you …"

"Help me, Sweet!"

The other faint whimpers had stopped. Did that mean the other dogs were …? No. Lucky could not let himself think about that. He howled just to break the silence.

"I think I can pull the cage out a bit," said Sweet. "Your door's loose, too. We might be able to get it open." Seizing the wire with her teeth, she tugged.

Lucky fought to keep himself calm. All he wanted to do was fling himself against the cage until it broke. His hindlegs kicked out wildly and he craned his head round, snapping at the wire. Sweet was gradually pulling the cage forward, stopping occasionally to scrabble at fallen stones with her paws.

"There. It's looser now. Wait while I …"

But Lucky could wait no longer. The cage door was torn at the upper corner, and he twisted until he could bite and claw at it. He worked his paw into the gap and pulled, hard.

The wire gave with a screech, just as Lucky felt a piercing stab in his paw pad – but the door now hung at an awkward angle. Wriggling and squirming, he pulled himself free and stood upright at last.

His tail was tight between his legs as tremors bolted through his skin and muscles. He and Sweet stared at the carnage and chaos around them. There were broken cages – and broken bodies. A small, smooth-coated dog lay on the ground nearby, lifeless, eyes dull. Beneath the last wall that had fallen, nothing stirred, but a limp paw poked out from between stones. The scent of death was already spreading through the Trap House air.

Sweet began to whimper with grief. "What was that? What happened?"

"I think – " Lucky's voice shook, and he tried again. "It was a Growl. I used to – my Mother-Dog used to tell me stories about the Earth-Dog, and the Growls she sent. I think the monster was a Big Growl ..."

"We have to get away from here!" There was terror in Sweet's whine.

"Yes." Lucky backed slowly away, shaking his head to dispel the death-smell. But it followed him, clinging to his nostrils.

He glanced around, desperate. Where the wall had tumbled on to the other dog cages, the broken blocks had collapsed into a pile, and light shone brightly through the haze of brick-dust and smoke.

"There, Sweet, where the stones have crumbled in. Come on!"

She needed no more urging, leaping up over the rubble. Aware of his wounded paw, Lucky picked his way more carefully, nervously glancing around for longpaws. Surely they'd come when they saw the destruction? Wouldn't they come and drag them back to the Trap House?

He shuddered, and quickened his pace, but even when he sprang down on to the street outside, following Sweet's lead, there was no sign of any longpaws.

Bewildered, he paused, and sniffed the air. It smelled so strange …

"Let's get away from the Trap House," he told Sweet in a low voice. "I don't know what's happened, but we should go far away in case the longpaws come back."

Sweet gave a sharp whine as her head drooped. "Lucky, I don't think there are any longpaws left."

Their journey was slow and silent. A sense of threat grew in Lucky's belly; so many of the roads and alleys he knew were blocked. Still he persevered, nosing his way around the broken buildings, through tangled, snaking coils torn from the ground. Despite what Sweet thought, Lucky was sure that the longpaws would return soon. He wanted to be far away from the destroyed Trap House when they did.

The sky was darkening by the time he felt they were far enough from the Trap House to rest; Lucky sensed that Sweet couldn't go much further anyway. Maybe Swift Dogs weren't as good at long journeys as they were at quick dashes. He gazed back the way they'd come, shadows lengthening across the ground, hiding spaces emerging in dark corners. Lucky shivered – what other animals might be out there, scared and hungry?

They were both exhausted from escaping the Big Growl. Sweet barely managed to tread her ritual sleep-circle before she slumped to the ground, laid her head on her forepaws and closed her troubled eyes. Lucky pressed himself close against her flank for warmth and comfort. *I'll stay awake for a while,* he thought, *Keep watch ... yes ...*

***

He woke with a start, shivering, his heart racing.

He'd slept no-sun away. His dreams were full of the distant rumbling of the Big Growl, the whining and beeping of loudcages and an endless line of longpaws running away from him. There was no sign of others here now. The city seemed abandoned.

Beneath the thorny scrub, Sweet slept on, the flanks of her sleek body gently rising and falling with each breath. Lucky stretched life back into his limbs.

Something about Sweet's deep sleep was comforting, but suddenly he needed more than the scented warmth of her sleeping body; he needed her awake and alert. He nuzzled Sweet's long face, licking her ears until she responded with a happy murmuring growl. She got to her feet, sniffing and licking him in return.

"How's that paw, Lucky?"

Her words instantly brought the sting back. Remembering the wound, he sniffed at his paw pad. An angry red mark scored the flesh, pulsing with pain. He licked it gently. It was closed, but only just, and he didn't want to make it bleed again.

"It's better, I think," he said, more hopefully than he felt; then, as they both slunk out from beneath the dense branches, his spirits slumped.

The road before them was broken, wildly tilted and cracked. Water sprayed high into the air from a long tube exposed by crumbling earth, making rainbows in the air. And it wasn't just here; in the sloping city streets, as far as Lucky could see, the light of the rising Sun-Dog glinted on tangled metal. A slick of water lay where he remembered that there had once been gardens, and the longpaw homes that used to seem tall and indestructible were now crumpled and slumped as if pummelled by a giant longpaw fist. The distant wail of broken loudcages went unanswered.

"The Big Growl," murmured Sweet, awestruck and afraid. "Look what it's done."

Lucky shivered. "You were right about the longpaws. There were packs and packs of them. Now I don't see a single one." He cocked his ears and tasted the air with his tongue: dust and an under-earth stink. No fresh scents. "Even the loudcages aren't moving."

Lucky tilted his head towards one of them, tipped on to its side, its snout half-buried in a collapsed wall. Light gleamed from its metal flanks but there was no roar and grumble; it seemed dead.

Sweet looked startled. "I always wondered what those were for. What did you call it?"

Lucky gave her a doubtful look. She didn't know what a loudcage was?

"Loudcages. You know – longpaws use them to get

about. They can't run as fast as we can."

He couldn't believe she didn't know this most basic detail about the longpaws. It gave him a bad feeling about setting out with her. Sweet's naivety wouldn't be much help when they were trying to survive.

Lucky sniffed the air again. The city's new smell made him uneasy. There was a rottenness, a lingering whiff of death and danger. *It doesn't smell like a home for dogs any more,* he thought.

He padded over to where water sprayed from a wound in the earth. In the sunken hole was an oily lake, its surface shimmering with rainbow colours. It gave off an odd smell that Lucky didn't like, but he was too thirsty to care, and lapped the water greedily, doing his best to ignore the foul taste. Beside him he saw Sweet's reflection as she also drank.

She was the first to lift her dripping muzzle, licking her pointed chops. "It's too quiet," she murmured. "We need to get out of this longpaw town." Sweet's fur lifted. "We should go to the hills. Find a wild place."

"We're as safe here as anywhere else," said Lucky. "We can use the old longpaw houses – maybe find food. And there are plenty of hiding places, believe me."

"Plenty of hiding places for other things, too," she retorted, bristling. "I don't like it."

"What do you have to be scared of?" Her legs looked long enough to race through high grasses and her frame was slender and light. "I bet you can run faster than anything!"

"Not around corners, I can't." She glanced nervously to the left and right. "And a city has lots of corners. I need space to run. That's where I can pick up speed."

Lucky scanned the area, too. She was right – the buildings crowded in on them. Maybe she had good reason to be edgy. "Let's at least keep moving. Some of those longpaws might still be close by, whether we can see them or not. I don't want to go back to the Trap House."

"Me neither," Sweet agreed, her lip curling to show her strong white teeth. "We should start looking for more dogs. We need a good, strong Pack!"

Lucky's muzzle wrinkled in doubt. He was not a Pack Dog. He had never understood what there was to like about living with a great mob of dogs, all dependent on one another, and having to submit to an Alpha. He didn't need anyone's help, and the last thing he wanted was someone who needed his. Just the thought of relying on other dogs made his skin prickle.

Obviously that isn't how Sweet feels, he thought. She was enthusiastic now, rattling off stories. "You would have loved my Pack! We ran together, and hunted together, catching rabbits and chasing rats ..." She became more subdued, and looked longingly towards the outskirts of the wrecked town. "Then the longpaws came and spoiled everything."

Lucky couldn't help responding to the sadness in her voice. "What happened?"

Sweet shook herself. "They rounded us up. So many of them, and all in the same brown fur! Staying together, that's what got us trapped, but – " Her growl grew fierce – "we wouldn't leave a single dog behind. That's Pack law. We stuck together, in good times and bad ..." Sweet paused, her dark eyes distant, unable to repress an unhappy whimper.

"Your Pack was with you in the Trap House," murmured Lucky sympathetically.

"Yes." She came to an abrupt halt. "Wait, Lucky, we have to go back!"

He darted in front of her as she spun round, blocking her way. "No, Sweet!'

"We *have* to!" Lucky scrambled sideways to stop her from slipping past him. "They're my Packmates. I can't leave until I find out what's happened to them! If any of them are still –"

"No, Sweet!" Lucky barked. "You saw how it was in

that place!"

"But we might have missed –"

"*Sweet.*" He tried a gentler tone, tentatively licking her unhappy face. "Back there, it's ruined. They're all dead, gone to the Earth-Dog. And we can't hang around here – the longpaws might come back ..."

That seemed to convince her. Sweet glanced back over her shoulder once more, then turned away again. With a deep sigh she began to walk on.

Lucky tried not to show his relief. He walked close beside her, their flanks brushing with every second step.

"Did you have friends in the Trap House too?" Sweet asked.

"Me?" said Lucky lightly, trying to cheer her up. "No thanks. I'm a Lone Dog."

Sweet gave him an odd glance. "There's no such thing. Every dog needs a Pack!"

"Not me. I like being on my own. I mean, I'm sure a Pack's best for some dogs," he added hurriedly to spare her feelings, "but I've walked alone since I left my Pup-Pack." He couldn't repress the proud lift of his head. "I can look after myself. There's no better place for a dog than the city. I'll show you! There's food for the finding, and warm crannies to sleep in, and shelter from the rain –"

But is that still true?

For a moment he hesitated, letting his eyes rove over the smashed streets, the shattered walls and broken clear-stones, the tilting roads and abandoned loudcages. *This isn't safe,* Lucky thought. *We need to get out of here as soon as we can.*

Not that he was going to share that fear with Sweet, not when she was already so anxious. If only there was some distraction –

There!

Lucky gave a high bark of excitement. They'd turned a corner, and there in front of them was a huge metal box, overturned in the middle of the road. Lucky scented – *food!*

He broke into a run, leaping in delight on to the side of the metal box. He'd seen longpaws throwing things they didn't want into these, locking them afterwards so that Lucky was never able to feast on the unwanted food. But now the box was on its side, the half-rotten contents spilled out across the ground. Black crows were hopping and jabbing around the piles. Lucky held his head high and barked as loud as he could. The crows cawed, alarmed, as they half-flapped away.

"Come on!" he yelled, springing into the stinking pile. Sweet followed, barking happily.

As Lucky nosed his way through the mound of scraps, he heard the dull fluttering of wings as the crows descended again. He leapt and snapped his jaws at an indignant bird and it rose into the air, its wings beating strongly.

Lucky sent a final snarl after the departing crow as he landed back on the ground, his paws skidding in the dirt. Immediately, his wounded paw howled with pain. It was like the fangs of the most vicious dog, biting all the way up his leg. He couldn't hold back his whimper of distress.

As Sweet dashed through the cloud of crows, chasing them clear, Lucky sat down and licked the pain away. He eagerly sniffed the air, enjoying the scent coming off the piles of discarded items that had spilled out across the ground. Contentment began to settle over him again, and he was distracted from his pain.

For a while the happy mood lingered, as Lucky and Sweet sniffed out the delicacies the crows had left. Sweet raked chicken bones from a cardboard bucket, and Lucky found a crust of bread, but the pickings were poor, especially after they'd worked up such an appetite.

"We're going to starve in this city." Sweet whined, licking an empty box that had once held some food. She held it down with one paw as she poked her nose inside.

"I promise we won't. It's not all scavenging." Lucky's

mind was flooded with an image of a place he used to visit. He nudged Sweet's flank affectionately. "I'll take you somewhere where we'll eat like Leashed Dogs."

Sweet's ears pricked up. "Really?"

"Really. This place will change your mind about cities."

Lucky trotted confidently down the road, his mouth already watering at the prospect of food. Sweet was right behind him. It was strange how happy he was with her company, how much he liked being able to help her. Usually he'd be itching for solitude by now, but ... he wasn't.

Maybe the Big Growl had changed more than just the city.

CHAPTER TWO

Sweet pressed close to Lucky's side as they walked through the deserted streets.

He had expected to see other dogs by now, and certainly a few longpaws. But the city was empty, and far too quiet. At least they had found a few stale scent-marks; that was reassuring. He stopped to sniff at an upturned bench that had been marked by a male Fierce Dog.

"They can't be far," Sweet interrupted his thoughts. She bent her muzzle to the scent, ears lifting. "This is a strong message. And there are others! Can't you smell them?"

The fur on Lucky's shoulders bristled: *why was Sweet so determined to find a Pack? Wasn't his company enough?*

"These dogs must be a long way away now," he said, backing away from the bench. "We won't catch up any time soon."

Sweet raised her nose in the air. "They smell nearby to me."

"But this only smells strong because it was their territory. They marked it over and over. I'm telling you, Sweet, they're far away already. I can pick out their scent in the distance."

"Really?" Sweet sounded doubtful again. "But I could catch up with them. I can catch anything!"

Why don't I just let her? Lucky wondered. *If she's so desperate to find a Pack, I should just tell her to run away as fast as she likes.*

Instead, he found himself rumbling a warning growl. "No, Sweet, you can't. Mustn't, I mean," he added quickly as she bristled. "You don't know the city; you could get lost."

Frustrated, Sweet cast her nose around in the air, then barked angrily. "Why did this happen, Lucky? I was fine before. My Pack was fine! We were so happy in the open country, and we didn't do any harm to the longpaws. If they'd only left us alone, if they hadn't rounded us up into that awful Trap House –"

She'd come to a miserable halt, and Lucky sat down beside her, wishing he could think of something to say. But he wasn't used to being responsible for another dog. Already it gave him an ache in his heart that he would rather live without.

He opened his jaws to try to reason with her some more, but stopped, gaping as a gang of fierce, furious creatures tumbled, yowling and squealing, into the street right in front of them.

Lucky felt fear tear through his hackles as his back stiffened. At first, he thought the fighting bundles of fur and teeth were sharpclaws, but then he realised they were different – very different. These animals were round and bushy-tailed – and they didn't hiss. They weren't dogs, and they weren't huge rats. Lucky gave an alarmed yelp, but the creatures didn't respond – they were too busy squabbling over a carcass that was so ripped and torn, he couldn't tell what it had once been.

Next to him, Sweet stood alertly, her eyes on the other animals. She took a moment to nuzzle his neck. "Don't worry about them, they won't hurt us."

"Are you sure?" asked Lucky. He'd caught sight of the face of one of them, a sinister black mask that seemed full of vicious little teeth.

"They're raccoons," Sweet replied. "We'll be fine if

we give them a wide berth. Try not to show too much interest and they won't feel threatened. I bet they're as hungry as we are."

Lucky followed Sweet's lead to the far sidewalk. She shot the raccoons a fierce bristling glare as she went. Lucky copied her, feeling prickles of anxiety in the roots of his fur.

We're not the only ones looking to fill our bellies, he realised. With everything torn from the ground and lying in ruins, easy pickings were a thing of the past. This was about survival now. He picked up his pace, keen to put as much space as he could between themselves and the raccoons.

A few streets beyond, Lucky tasted familiar air and gave a happy bark. It was the alley he'd been looking for! He ran forward a few paces, then sat down and scratched at his ear with a hindpaw, enjoying the moment, anticipating Sweet's delight. The delicious smell of food was getting stronger. Here, at least, he could guarantee a meal.

"Come on!" he yipped. "I promise, you won't regret this."

She padded up behind him and cocked her head quizzically. "What is this place?"

He nodded at the panes of clear-stone. There were

long tubes there. Normally, they breathed chicken-scented steam into the air – but not today. Still, this was definitely the right place. Excited, he turned a couple of circles, tail wagging quickly.

"It's a Food House. A place where longpaws give food to other longpaws!"

"But we're not longpaws," she pointed out. "Who's going to give food to us?"

"Just you watch." Lucky jumped forward mischievously, dodging around tumbled bins and a small heap of rubble. He tried not to think about how ruined everything was, or that they hadn't seen a single longpaw walking the streets. "We'll do what Old Hunter does. He's the expert!"

Sweet brightened. "Old Hunter? Is he a Packmate of yours?"

"I told you, I don't have a Pack. Old Hunter is just a *friend*. Even Lone Dogs can find hunting mates, you know! Watch this. Copy what I do ..."

It was such an easy method of getting food, and it took no time to learn – Lucky was pleased to be able to teach Sweet something. He sat back on his haunches, tilted his head, and let his tongue loll out.

Sweet slowly slinked around him, studying the posture. Her head cocked. "I don't understand," she whined.

"Just trust me," Lucky growled.

Sweet whined again, then turned to sit down beside Lucky as she did her best to copy him.

"That's it!" Lucky barked. "Now, lift one ear a little higher. Like this, see? And a friendly mouth – look hungry but hopeful! You got it!"

Lucky wagged his tail as he gave Sweet an affectionate nudge with his muzzle. Then he turned his attention back to the Food House door, and waited. A longpaw would spot them soon. Slow moments passed and Lucky's tail began to wag more and more slowly until it came to rest in the dust. The door stayed resolutely shut, so Lucky padded over to scratch at it. Still no reply. He gave a small respectful whine.

"How long do we stay like this? It's a bit – undignified," said Sweet. She licked her chops, then let her tongue hang out again.

"I don't understand..." Lucky's tail drooped down in embarrassment. Where was his friendly longpaw? Surely he hadn't run from the Big Growl. Lucky scratched at the door again, but still there was no reply.

Sweet's nose was back in the air. "I don't think it's working."

"The longpaws must be busy, that's all," Lucky

grumbled. "This is an important place for them. They wouldn't have just *left*." He tried not to notice how high and anxious his voice had become. He trotted around to the back of some bins and spoil-boxes and scratched his way through to a side door. Up on his hindlegs, he put his paws against the wood, and felt it sag and creak.

"Look! The Food House is broken." He tugged at a sagging hinge with his teeth. "That's why the longpaws are busy. Come on, Sweet!"

The Food House smells must have been enticing enough to make Sweet forget her doubts, because she helped him nose and pull and tug at the broken door until it cracked open. Lucky wriggled through ahead of her, his tail thrashing in anticipation of scrumptious food.

He slowed, glancing from side to side. This room was a strange place that he hadn't seen before, lined with huge metal boxes. There were snaking, shiny lengths of what looked like long worms. Lucky knew that these usually hummed with the longpaws' invisible energy. But nothing hummed now. Above him, water dripped from the collapsed roof, and broad cracks ran along the walls.

There was a blurred reflection of himself and Sweet in the big steel boxes. A shudder passed over him to see how distorted their faces were. The food smell was strong now, but old, and Lucky felt prickles of uncertainty.

"I don't like this," said Sweet in a low voice.

Lucky whined his agreement. "This isn't the way it normally is. But it should be fine. It's probably just a little bit of damage from the Big Growl." Tentatively Lucky pushed on through the rubble and mess. Sweet watched him, her muzzle wrinkling with uncertainty. "Don't look like that," he told her. "Come on!"

She lifted her slender paws high as she moved around broken, splintered shards of white stone that covered the floor.

There was another door, but it was easy to push open – almost too easy, because it swung wildly back and forth, almost bumping Sweet's roving nose and making her jump. As it grew still again, Lucky sniffed the air.

The chaos was even worse in here, beyond the room of metal boxes; longpaw stuff was flung in heaps, sitting-boxes broken and listing together, thick dust falling from the broken walls to cover everything. Shivers rippled through Lucky's fur.

Abruptly he stopped, drawing his lips back from his teeth. *What's that smell? I know it, but ...* He couldn't repress a frightened growl. Something moved in the corner.

Lucky took a few hesitant paces, crouching low to the ground. The scent felt strong inside his nose. He bounded forward and pawed at the fallen roof beams. There was someone here!

White dust stirred and swirled; Lucky heard a groan, and a breathless rasping of longpaw words. He recognised only one. "Lucky ..."

The voice was weak, but it was familiar. Whimpering, Lucky sank his teeth into one of the huge broken beams and leaned his weight back on his paws, heaving. His whole body trembled with the effort, and he could feel his teeth being pulled from his jaws. It was no good! He released his bite and fell back, panting with the effort. The longpaw lay still and unmoving beneath the beam, a trickle of dried blood tracking down his face.

Lucky drew closer, ignoring his instincts, which were telling him to run away as fast as he could. Behind him, he could hear Sweet pacing with anxiety. Lucky lowered his head over the longpaw's body. One arm was free of the rubble, twisted at an unnatural angle. The longpaw's face was as pale as snow, his lips a horribly unnatural blue, but they curved in a smile as his eyes met Lucky's.

He's alive! Lucky licked at his nose and cheeks, gently clearing some of the coating of dust. If Lucky could just clean the longpaw up, he'd look much healthier – just like his old self. But as Lucky stepped back, he saw that the skin beneath the dust was grey. The longpaw's ragged breath was the faintest of whispers, barely stirring the fur on Lucky's muzzle.

The longpaw's eyes flickered open, and with a groan of pain he lifted his trembling free hand to pat Lucky's head. Lucky nuzzled and licked him again, but the hand fell away, and the eyes closed once more.

"Wake up, longpaw," Lucky whined softly, his tongue lashing the cold, pale face. "Wake up ..."

Lucky waited. But the lips were still and cold.

The whisper of breath was gone.

CHAPTER THREE

A yelp of despair shattered the silence. Turning hurriedly away from the dead longpaw, Lucky stared at Sweet. Every hair on her sleek coat seemed to bristle with fear. Stiff-legged, she backed away, tail tight between her legs.

"I don't want your city!" she whined. "There's death and danger *everywhere*. I can't stand it!"

She let loose a howl of disgust and sprinted, making the door swing wildly once again as she shot through it. Lucky scrambled after her, knowing he had no hope of catching a Swift Dog.

But Sweet's speed did her no favours in the close quarters of the steel room. She was hemmed in, dashing desperately from reflection to distorted reflection, crashing wildly into the metal boxes and skidding on the slick floor. When she slammed into a wall in her terror, Lucky lunged forward and pinned her to the ground.

She squirmed beneath him, panicking, but Lucky kept his forepaws firmly on her sweating flank, his eyes fixed on hers. "Calm down! You're going to hurt yourself."

"I can't stay ..."

As Sweet's barks fell away to anxious pants, Lucky let his weight gently flop down on her. "It's nothing to be scared of, Sweet. He's only dead." He repeated what he was sure she already knew, hoping to calm her. "It's a natural smell: the longpaw's life-force. Just like when we die – our selves leave our bodies, become part of the world."

Lucky had been taught ever since he was a pup that that was the way of life and death. When a dog met his end and his body went to the Earth Dog, his self floated up to meet all the scents of the air, to mingle with them and become part of the whole world. That's what was happening to the longpaw now, Lucky was certain.

Sweet's flanks stopped heaving as her panting breaths subsided. Lucky could still see the whites of her wide, fearful eyes. He cautiously released her and she climbed to her feet. "I know that," she growled. "But

I don't want to be anywhere near escaping longpaw spirits. I want to find as many other dogs as we can. We need to track down more survivors, and get us all out of here *right now!*"

"But there's nothing we need to get away from – nothing will hurt us now, Sweet. The Food House fell on the longpaw in the Big Growl, that's all ..." Lucky needed Sweet to trust him. If he could reassure her, perhaps all of this would make sense to Lucky too.

"Where are the other longpaws?" Sweet barked, tossing her head. "They've either run away or they're dead, Lucky! We should leave this city, and find a Pack!"

Lucky opened his mouth to speak, but the words dried up in his throat. He could only stare at her sadly. Sweet half-turned to leave, then froze with one paw raised and all her muscles tensed, eager to flee. She gazed at Lucky for a long moment, licking her lips uncertainly. "Aren't you coming with me?"

Lucky hesitated. The idea of a Pack didn't appeal to him one bit, but – for some reason – he didn't want Sweet to leave. He liked having her around. For the first time, he felt himself tremble at the prospect of being alone. And she was waiting for him, ears pricked, eyes hopeful ...

He shook himself. He'd spent his whole life on these

streets. That's what he was – a Lone Dog.

"I can't."

"But you can't stay here!" Sweet howled.

"I told you: I'm not a Pack Dog. I never will be."

She gave a sharp bark of exasperation. "Dogs aren't meant to be alone!"

Lucky gave her a regretful look. "*I* am."

Sweet sighed, and padded back to him. Fondly she licked his face. Lucky nuzzled her in response, fighting down a mournful whine that wanted to erupt from his belly.

"I'll miss you," she said quietly. Then she turned to wriggle through the door.

Lucky padded forward. "You don't have to …" But with a flash of her tail, she was gone. Lucky found himself staring at an empty space.

For a while, Lucky didn't feel like moving. He settled down on his belly, chin resting on his forepaws as he listened to the click of Sweet's claws on the ground, fading into the ruined emptiness of the streets. Even when he could hear her no longer, her scent still clung to the air. He wished it would vanish – and take this terrible pang of loneliness with it.

Lucky shut his eyes and tried to focus his mind on other things.

But that just left the hunger.

It was like a set of sharp teeth, gnawing and chewing at his stomach. Lucky was almost relieved to feel the pain – at least it took his mind off Sweet. *That's why I don't let myself get close to other dogs,* he thought.

Back in the room with the dead longpaw, Lucky sniffed and scratched in every corner, licking at crumbs and grease. Some of the broken things on the floor held smears of food, so he lapped at them, trying not to cut his tongue; then he leapt on to one of the un-toppled tables to find small scraps to nibble on. There was so little, and the tantalizing taste of it only made his stomach growl louder, the teeth bite harder. He didn't go near the longpaw, forced himself not to look.

I'm on my own now. That's the way it should be.

The steel room would have food, he was sure – that was what must be in the metal boxes lined up around the walls. But when he scratched at them, they refused to open. Whimpering in hunger, he tugged and bit at the metal doors. They stuck firm. He flung his body against them. Nothing. It was no use: he was going to have to wander further, see what else he could find.

At least he'd be in the open air again, he thought: free and easy, the way he used to be. He had looked after himself just fine until now – and he would keep on doing that.

Lucky headed back out into the alleyway. It seemed so much emptier than before, and he found himself scampering as fast as he could across the rubble, until he reached the broad open space beyond. Surely he'd find something here? It had always been such a bustle of noise and energy, busy with longpaws and their loudcages.

There were plenty of loudcages here, sure enough, but none of them were moving and there was still not a longpaw in sight, friendly or otherwise. Some of the loudcages had fallen on to their flanks – a big one had crashed its blunt snout into an empty space in the wall of a building, shattered pieces of clear-stone glittering. Picking his way carefully through the shards, Lucky felt his hackles rise. The scent of longpaw was back in the air, but it was not comforting: it was the scent that had settled on the Food House owner when he had grown still. The silence was oppressive, punctuated only by the steady drip and trickle of water.

Above him the Sun-Dog, which had been so high and bright, was casting long shadows from the buildings that had withstood the Big Growl. Each time he passed through one of the pools of darkness, Lucky shivered and hurried back into the light. He kept moving, the patches of light growing steadily smaller, the shadows longer, and the ache of hunger in his belly sharper.

Maybe I should have gone with Sweet …

No. There was no point thinking that way. He was a Lone Dog again, and that was *good.*

He turned and trotted determinedly down another alley. This was his city! There was always food and comfort to be had here. Even if he had to dig deep for the leftovers in Food House spoil-boxes, or find another overturned smell-box in the road, there would be something the crows and the rats hadn't found. He was self-reliant, independent Lucky.

He was not going to starve.

Lucky drew to a stop as he got his bearings. This alley wasn't as damaged by the Big Growl as other places, but there was one deep, vicious crack running up the middle of it, and two spoil-boxes had been knocked flying. There might be a real feast there, if he rummaged. Lucky bounded up to the nearest one – then froze, nerves crackling beneath his fur. The scent was sharp and strong, and he knew it well.

Enemy!

Lips peeling back from his teeth, he sniffed the air to pinpoint the creature. Above him was a set of slender steps going up a wall, and his instincts pulled his eyes, ears and nose towards it: that was the kind of place where this enemy liked to lurk, ready to pounce, needle-claws raking.

There it was: striped fur bristling, pointed ears laid flat, and tiny glinting fangs bared. Its low, threatening growl was punctuated by vicious hissing as it crouched, every muscle taut for its attack.

Sharpclaw!

CHAPTER FOUR

The green-yellow eyes glared down at Lucky with that dangerous mixture of fear and malice he remembered so well. He fought to suppress the tight ball of nerves in his belly even as his neck-fur lifted. The sharpclaw would smell fear, he knew that; it would sense any hesitation – but Lucky would not hesitate.

His lips pulled back from his teeth and he raised his head to bark the most ferocious bark he could muster.

I'm dangerous too, sharpclaw …

It got to its feet, stiff-legged and swollen to what seemed like twice its size, fur standing on end all over its arched body. One paw almost lifted, claws unsheathed and ready to strike. Lucky told himself not to look away and trained his gaze determinedly on the other animal, deepening his snarl.

Its growling and hissing were ferocious now, and Lucky felt sharpclaw-spit land on his nose. The creature launched itself from the rickety ladder, and Lucky forced himself to hold his ground as the sharpclaw landed lightly, perfectly, on a half-wrecked loudcage. It drew itself up with a lethal glare.

And then the loudcage woke up.

Raucous wails ripped the air as it screamed and howled, flashing its orange eyes and its white ones. For an instant, both Lucky and the sharpclaw were startled into frozen silence. Then, at the same instant, they bolted.

Panic lent Lucky speed, despite his injured paw, but it made him breathless, too. He found himself yelping as he ran, the shriek of the loudcage almost drowning him out. Careening around a corner, Lucky raced as hard as he could away from loudcages and high buildings.

There in his path stood another sharpclaw. It was as black as no-sun, and as rigid as a tree.

Lucky didn't even slow down. The sharpclaw's ears flattened and it opened its mouth in a snarl. Lucky darted to one side, racing around it, growling, his hackles up. He had to end this fight – quickly. He launched himself into the air, landing on his enemy. Almost immediately, he lost his footing and found himself tumbling with the sharpclaw, who yowled in panic. One flailing claw caught Lucky's shoulder with a glancing scratch.

Rolling to his feet, paws scrabbling, he saw the black sharpclaw racing down a nearby alley. It had clearly decided escape was more important than fighting – Lucky's attack had worked, however fumbling. Panting, his legs trembling beneath him, Lucky blinked and listened to the silence. The loudcage had stopped howling.

Well, *of course* it had. They always did in the end.

Lucky felt a pang of hurt pride as his flanks twitched and calmed. Lucky – Lone Dog, Street Dog, City Dog – scared of a loudcage howl! He was glad Old Hunter hadn't witnessed *that!* But he quickly shook it off. That was the reflex of a proper Lone Dog. The moment's slight embarrassment gave way to pride. He was still on his paw-tips, smart and streetwise as ever. No Growl, Big or Small, could take that away from him.

Lucky felt his muscles stop shivering. He trotted on; this road seemed to lead away from the once-crowded centre, and that was a good direction for the moment. It was his own decision, his own choice; one of the big advantages of being a Lone Dog.

Lucky glanced around with curiosity as he walked towards the edge of the city where most of the longpaws lived; it didn't seem quite as bad here. There wasn't so much to shatter; these longpaw houses didn't have as far to topple.

At last he stopped, turning a circle and eyeing his surroundings. This was one of those streets where longpaws lived and slept. And it wasn't the kind where the longpaws lived piled on top of one another in stone cages ... no, here the longpaw houses were set in neat little squares of garden that were full of intriguing smells. And the most intriguing of them all was ...

Lucky opened his jaws, pricked his ears, eagerly sniffed the air. Elusive but distinct, the scent made his stomach churn with anticipation. *Food!*

He bounded towards its source. Meat! Meat was cooking on one of those metal longpaw fire-boxes! The invisible fires that made the raw meat turn dark, that made the food smell so strong and tangy and ...

A bird clattered from a tree with a flap of black wings, bringing him to a startled halt. He needed to slow down. Hunger should not make him reckless. He knew from experience, not every longpaw was friendly when it came to food. Some of them were reluctant to share, protecting their food the way Mother-Dogs protected their pups.

Still, he wasn't about to give up altogether. At a more cautious pace he padded forward, his fur bristling all over with longing. He could almost taste the food now, feel it filling his belly, warm and satisfying. Not far now! *Not far!*

He paused in the shadow of a stunted tree, his tongue lolling, jaw wide and grinning, his tail thumping the ground hard and fast. There it was: a rundown wooden longpaw house, set in overgrown grass and shaded by straggly branches. And there was the fire-box, gently sizzling and steaming. And there was the longpaw – well-fed, by the look of him, with a belly that bulged right through his fur.

And there – also looking well-fed – was his Fierce Dog.

They were both snoozing in the shade, the longpaw sprawled on a raised surface by the fire-box, the Fierce Dog lying at his feet. Lucky knew its kind from many a food-scrap. It wasn't very big, but it was deep-chested and heavy-jawed and, probably, short-tempered.

But maybe this one would be happy to share?

Lucky hesitated, catching a tiny whine in his throat. The food-smell was so tempting, but ...

Why were they here? Weren't all the longpaws gone,

or dead, like the friendly one in the Food House? Why hadn't this longpaw left too? Dozing beneath the Sun-Dog like this, he seemed not to have noticed the Big Growl at all.

Or maybe this longpaw was dead, and so was his Fierce Dog? Lucky sniffed the air uncertainly. The strong tang of grilling meat could have been masking the death-smell…

Warily, Lucky took a pace forward, then two, his tail raised, his muzzle dripping with eagerness. He licked his chops. Neither the longpaw nor his dog moved.

He had to try. Close to the fire-box now, Lucky eyed a chunk of sizzling meat. The distance and angle were just about right…

He lunged.

The longpaw's eyes flew open, and he leapt to his feet, brandishing a stick. His barks stung Lucky's ears. The Fierce Dog had woken too, springing to the attack position, legs stiff as he unleashed a furious volley of fight-barks.

"GET BACK! It's MINE! Want to fight me for it? FIGHT ME OR *RUN!*"

Lucky was no match for the longpaw's stick, let alone for the Fierce Dog and its savage jaws. Turning tail, he bolted from the garden, sharp terror overwhelming the gnawing ache of hunger.

He leapt a crumbling wall and raced down the hard road. He was sure the Fierce Dog must be chasing him, but he didn't dare turn to look. If the Fierce Dog caught him, he wouldn't stand a chance. His paws skidded on the broken and uneven ground, almost tripping him. Panting, heart thrashing, fear biting hard at his guts, he bolted along a road that seemed never to end.

Until it did.

Blackness opened before him. He automatically flung his weight sideways, halting his momentum, his haunches scraping painfully on the rough road surface. His claws rattled against unyielding stone, his tail lashed over hideous emptiness, and at last he stopped, aching with terror and pain. His injured paw throbbed with each beat of his heart and Lucky was sure the wound had opened again.

He raised his head. He was lying on his flank on the brink of a vast black hole in the earth. He scrambled to his feet and lowered his head to sniff fearfully at the crack in the road. It was wider than he was long, and the bottom was hidden by shadows thicker than clouds.

Bristling, he took a nervous step away, then shook himself, and risked another look. Was Earth-Dog down there, waiting for him as she once waited for Lightning? Would she spring suddenly from the darkness and drag him down? He was almost afraid to look harder, but he found it hard to believe that Earth-Dog had let the Big Growl happen. Why would she let it destroy her own home? Perhaps Earth-Dog, too, was afraid of the Growl …

Lucky found himself trembling, but there was no movement from within the black depths, no sinister snarling. Breathing deeply, he paced along the edge, feeling his courage return.

He had to get around this hole. He loped first one way along its edge, then the other. Panic began to rise in his chest again. There was no end to the hole: it extended through gardens as far as he could see in both directions. Even a longpaw house had collapsed into it, leaving rooms on each side open to the sky. Back and forth he ran again, yipping with desperation.

He didn't dare go much further; there were trees ahead that obscured his view of the crack, but they were distant, and as far as he could see the gap only seemed to get wider. It was too big a risk. Street Dogs were more sensible than that.

Then, not far enough in the distance, he heard the Fierce Dog's voice.

"You! *Food-stealer!* I'll teach you a lesson! *Come*

back and try that again!"

Lucky stood still, pricking his ears towards the furious barking. Thank the Sky-Dogs his new enemy liked to talk so much; if it had more breath to spare it might have caught him by now. But it was going to catch him soon …

There was nothing else he could do. Lucky hurtled back the way he'd come, hearing his pursuer lumbering closer all the time. He had to give himself a good run-up, because he would only get one chance to clear this chasm.

He had to hope he could live up to his name.

He spun to face the opening again, and began to race. Faster and faster, his paws flew across the ground. As the bottomless crack opened before him, he launched himself from the edge. Now, there was nothing below his belly but death and blackness …

The Earth-Dog waiting to swallow him …

He landed hard. He tumbled and rolled, welcoming the pain he felt in his paw and bones. He was alive!

For long moments he let himself lie there, his flanks heaving as he shut his eyes and felt the deep relief flood him. There was no way the stocky Fierce Dog could clear that great rip in the earth. He was safe!

Safe … but starving.

Lucky's hunger returned, as painful as being kicked in the gut by a cruel longpaw.

Desperate and miserable, he laid his head on his paws and whimpered softly to himself. He was alone. Alone, lost, and scared.

Maybe he should have gone with Sweet …

But then what? They might *both* be starving by now, and he'd have a second belly to fill. This way, Lucky had only himself to look after. And he had always been good at that.

As he rose to a shaky standing position, his ears were low and his tail was between his legs. He needed food, and soon. The shadows had lengthened even more, swallowing the last patches of light; the blackness of no-sun would soon be here, and he knew he shouldn't stay in the open.

Slowly, painfully, he slunk into an alley and began to hunt for a sleeping-place. As he sniffed at doors and gaps in the rubble, he couldn't help thinking about that terrible void in the Earth. Had Sweet come upon such a crack? He hoped she hadn't slipped into the Earth's jaws, as he nearly had …

He crossed three separate roads, all the while limping badly, before he finally found a wrecked loudcage whose door hung loose. Lucky barely had the strength to haul himself into it, but he was rewarded with a scrap of shiny silver paper that smelled of food. It felt tinny and strange against his teeth, but when he peeled it open there was a piece of stale bread with old-smelling meat tucked inside. A longpaw had taken a bite of it, no more.

It was no fire-box steak, but it would calm the raging hunger just a little. Gratefully, Lucky wolfed it down, then licked and chewed the last scraps from the paper, not caring that he was swallowing bits of that as well.

Lucky raised his head and closed his eyes, quietly thanking the Sky-Dogs for that small morsel of luck. Feeling a little better, he paced a tiny circle on the loudcage's back seat in his familiar sleep-ritual, then curled up, tucking his tail around him.

Please, Earth-Dog, keep the Big Growl silent this no-sun.

Settling his head on his forelegs, he licked as well as he could at his sore paw until sleep overwhelmed him.

CHAPTER FIVE

That sound … what was it …? The Big Growl – back to finish him off?

The noise filled his skull, stung his ears, made his head ache. Not just the howling and snarling that seemed to echo from every direction; worse, there was the savage ripping of flesh, the snap of vicious jaws.

The sound of dogs, fighting. Fighting to the death …

Could it be the Storm of Dogs? Was it here? No, it couldn't be – it couldn't –

Pressing himself to the ground, lowering his ears, Lucky whimpered his fear and horror. It was coming to swamp him. Just like the Big Growl. There was no escape. He had to turn and face the Storm, and fight for his life –

But as he leapt to his paws and spun to face the savage warrior hounds, he saw – nothing. Nothing but more darkness, emptiness; as gaping a void as the hole in the earth that he'd leapt.

And all he could hear was a distant, fading, terrifying howl …

***

He woke with a start. *Sweet!*

No. Sweet wasn't here now.

And it was a dream. The Storm of Dogs had been nothing but a dream … except that it had felt so real. Sounded and smelled so real. Was it hunger-madness, or was it worse than that – a vision of something that was yet to come …?

Nonsense. He couldn't afford to think of such things. Tired and stiff and sore, Lucky recognised the hiding place he'd crawled into last night. It smelled of hot metal, of tanned hide and the strange juice the longpaws fed their loudcages. The Sun-Dog was shining, but for a moment he still missed the warmth of Sweet at his back. The loneliness felt like a great stone in his belly. For a moment he wanted to bay his misery out loud to the empty blue sky.

He didn't know where he was, or where he was going. Perhaps even a Lone Dog sometimes needed a travelling companion: someone to hunt with, sleep beside, someone to watch his back. Someone he too could protect.

No. He walked *alone,* and he liked it.

The heat in the loudcage was growing stifling, his hunger unbearable. Slinking out, he glanced once in each direction, then set off hesitantly down the side street. And just at that moment, something black took off above his head with a clatter of wings.

Pausing to pant and lick his dry chops, Lucky stared up at the crow; it didn't fly far. It flapped and perched on a broken metal pipe that led down from the roof of the longpaw home. There must have been water caught there, because it dipped its black beak to the pipe and drank. Then it cocked its head and eyed him directly.

It was just like the crow that had flown out of the tree yesterday, warning Lucky to be careful. It might even be the same one.

Don't be silly. All crows look the same! Lucky scolded himself. Still … that crow yesterday had appeared at just the right moment, or he'd have run headlong into the jaws of the Fierce Dog. Maybe it had been sent by the Sky-Dogs to warn him; it certainly seemed to be watching him very closely. He raised his gaze to the bird's, and yipped with respect.

It tilted its head to the other side, gave a caw, and flapped lazily away.

Half sorry to see the bird go, half glad it wasn't staring at him any longer, Lucky set off again, taking a shortcut through the narrowest of alleys and emerging on to a broad avenue. On either side were large longpaw homes that had crumbled into piles of dust and rock. The power of the Big Growl was displayed here for any dog to fear.

One longpaw house had had its roof sliced off. It now lay in front of it like a scrap of unwanted food. Two trees tilted crazily against each other, as if they were trying to wrestle. Around the next corner, another longpaw house had collapsed in on itself, and Lucky stiffened, backing away, his hackles rising and skin quivering. The smell of death was strong here.

Distracted and unsettled by the scent, Lucky stumbled in a hole in the ground, jarring his sore paw. As he tried to lick it better, a sound burst from the city silence made him yelp with shock and dash for cover, forgetting the throb of pain. The noise was like a loudcage, but different – deeper, a resounding growl. Peering out from his hiding place between two tipped spoil-boxes, Lucky shivered and watched the street as the rumbling roar grew louder and louder – and stopped.

If this was a loudcage it was an Alpha. He had never seen one so huge and threatening, its flanks a dull green metal that looked strong and indestructible.

A door creaked open, and a longpaw stepped out.

Lucky felt his heart quicken. Had the Big Growl changed even the longpaws? Because this was like no longpaw he'd seen before. It moved like a longpaw, and smelled – vaguely – like a longpaw, but it was covered from top to toe in the strangest fur that Lucky had ever seen – a bright yellow that made Lucky's eyes water. Its face was blank, black and flat.

There were tremors in Lucky's skin, but he was almost certain this was a longpaw. And who was to say it was a hostile one? He'd long ago discovered you couldn't tell with longpaws. A dog just had to approach with caution, and not be too proud to run away if necessary.

He crept from his hiding place, slinking low to the ground with his tail tucked between his legs, and looked beseechingly up at the blank, eyeless face. The longpaw didn't immediately kick him, so Lucky let his tongue hang out, and pricked his ears, hopefully.

It glanced down at him. There was no food in its thickly covered hands, only a strange stick that bleeped, so things did not look promising – and sure enough the longpaw muttered some words in its language and swiped its arm, a gesture that Lucky knew meant, *Go away.*

It didn't sound very welcoming, but it didn't sound very hostile, either. It certainly didn't try to collar him with a long stick, so it couldn't be from the Trap House. Lucky gave it a hopeful whine.

It waved him away again, its tone harsher.

Certainly it was a longpaw, because it spoke like one, but there was no way of smelling its intentions beneath that strange fur. And Lucky couldn't read that eyeless face. *I guess I should give up.* He backed off, and loped back into the alley. It was strange. He'd sensed neither friendliness nor hostility from the longpaw – just a deep nervous tension. This wasn't the way that longpaws normally were.

The sound of the loudcage rumbling back into life sent fear down his spine again, and he ran, heading for the centre of the city, where he knew most longpaws prowled. He tended to avoid these particular streets if he could. Usually there was nothing but noise: the constant growl of loudcages, longpaws barking into the small machines they held at their ear. But as he approached, the only thing Lucky heard was the moan of wind between buildings, the drip of water, the creak and groan of roofs and metal bent to breaking point.

In front of him the road was covered with tiny glittering pieces of clear-stone, and Lucky stopped. He knew he couldn't afford another cut paw. Instead he looked up at the building that had shattered in the Growl.

It had once been made of huge sheets of clear-stone; now its face was open to the still air. He started when he saw longpaws staring from the base, but then he remembered that these were fake longpaws, with no smell, no warmth, no movement. Cautiously he paced between them, sniffing at their brand-new furs; even those didn't smell of longpaw. Some of them had been stripped of their fur and knocked sideways, but they weren't hurt. They stared at him, empty-eyed.

Lucky slunk warily between the stiff and lifeless longpaws, but their eyes didn't blink and their skin smelled of nothing. This place was what they called their *mall*. Longpaws – real ones – had gone in and out of this building all the time, he remembered. Sometimes they'd carried food, but they'd never stopped to give him any. And when he'd tried to saunter in to find the Food Houses for himself, he'd been chased out by other longpaws, who all wore the same blue fur. He remembered all too well having to dodge their kicks.

But there were no angry longpaws to stop him now!

Lucky sniffed. Once this place had been a confusion of scents: cold air that blew like a constant wind through the rooms; strong unpleasant odours that the longpaws sprayed on themselves; strange sharp smells smeared on the floors by longpaws with long wooden poles that ended in a ball of rags. And there had been the new-made scent of untouched things set out for longpaws to gaze at. Those smells had mostly faded, and the clingy warm air of Outside had forced its way in. That, and the death-smell that haunted the whole city. Lucky shuddered. He had never smelled so much death before; even the Earth-Dog would be offended by so strong a sense of ended lives.

He shook himself free of the horror. There was more than all that. There was food!

It smelled stale and maybe a little spoiled, but Lucky didn't care. Keeping a nervous eye open for the longpaws in blue, he made his way further into the building. There were more broken clear-stones here, littering the smooth, shiny floor, and he was careful to avoid them, but he couldn't help staring at the deserted longpaw houses within the huge mall. Some seemed untouched; others had been stripped bare. In some places, piles of longpaw stuff lay abandoned. Lucky could smell both longpaw and dog, but the strong stench of fear and desperation overlaid both. His neck prickled.

Ah! he thought, pausing to sniff at a ransacked heap of bags made out of some kind of old preserved skin. They were polished, and not fresh, but the smell was strong and familiar. Longpaws carried their things in bags and pouches like these. Perhaps this was a place where they kept their precious things – like burying bones! They left them here, piled together, and came back for them later. Was that it? Longpaws had been here since the Big Growl, he was almost certain, taking the things away; he could see scuff marks on the floor from their covered feet. Apart from the skin-pouches, and some of the furs, nothing else looked familiar. The smell of food was growing stronger, so Lucky headed towards it, taking little notice of the racks of sparkling longpaw collars and studs, the scraps of longpaw-fur hanging on plastic hooks, the stacks of paper and boxes. He even caught sight of a row of small imitation dogs, as unmoving and lifeless as the strange-smelling longpaws at the front of the building.

The rich scent of food was coming from above. Hesitantly he put his good paw on a ragged metal hill that led upwards. It seemed to bear his weight, so he took a step or two further; then he was suddenly too hungry and eager to be cautious. Taking a deep breath, he bounded as fast as he could up the metal hill. There were grooves on it that felt odd beneath his paw pads, especially the wounded one, but he made it without mishap to the top.

And drew to a stop.

That wasn't only food ... there was a dog-scent that seemed familiar, too: a musk of well-known sweat and skin and breath.

Old Hunter!

Lucky's heart leapt. He could hardly believe there might be friendly company ahead; there was no one he'd be happier to see right now. Lucky dodged and slunk through the longpaw sitting-boxes and small tables spilled across the floor as he followed his nose. The food-scent was strong now, reminding him of those things the longpaws ate – meat chopped up and made into round shapes like flattened balls; the discs that were smothered in tomatoes and cheese and spicy chopped meat. The smells were stale and old, but his chops watered just thinking about the prospects.

Clambering clear of the last tangle of longpaw sitting boxes, Lucky stood and sniffed. There were openings in the wall, but they were covered by metal shutters. In one of the gaps, though, the metal was torn sideways, sagging, and it smelt strongly of meat. Lucky would have bolted straight for it – if it hadn't been for the low growling coming from below the counter.

But there was nothing to fear. If he'd been unsure about the smell, the tone of that growl had definitely convinced him.

Happily Lucky sprang up on to the counter, wobbling a little on his sore paw.

"Old Hunter!"

Lucky leaned down on his forepaws and lowered his shoulders and his head, opening his mouth and panting. Even if Old Hunter was a friend, it was best to look unthreatening.

Old Hunter's blunt muzzle was slightly curled as he stared up. He rose, standing tall on his powerful legs, and growled.

Then he sprang for Lucky's throat.

CHAPTER SIX

Lucky yelped in shock as he tumbled backwards under the big dog's attack. Old Hunter stood over him, snarling. Lucky made himself lie still and submissive as drool from Old Hunter's jaws dripped on to his muzzle. Lucky whined softly, and a light of recognition dawned suddenly in Old Hunter's eyes.

"*Lucky?*"

Feeling a dizzy wave of relief, Lucky thumped his tail eagerly. The big stocky dog above him stepped away, relaxing and pricking his ears. He sniffed once more at Lucky's face, then grinned, panting.

"Lucky!" Old Hunter snuffled and licked affection-ately at Lucky's ears as the smaller dog scrambled to his feet, trying not to slide off the countertop. "I didn't recognise you. You *stink*, my friend!"

Lucky yipped with delight. "I've been hunting."

Old Hunter wrinkled his muzzle. "Mostly in spoilboxes, by the smell of you."

"There wasn't much else." Lucky's ears drooped, then he pricked them up again. "It's so good to see you!" *It really was*, he thought. Not that he'd been desperate for company, of course. If he hadn't run into Old Hunter it would have made no difference to him – but now that he *had*, well … it felt better than he expected.

"It's good to see you, too. It's been a long time." All the same, there was a certain wariness in the big dog's eyes as he leapt back down to the meat scattered on the floor.

"Too long," said Lucky. "I'm ready to see a friend again!" He hesitated, not wanting to sound needy or weak in front of this independent old dog. "We can watch each other's backs, at least! Maybe now I can get a few bites of food without looking over my shoulder."

The excitement – and the sight and smell of the meat littered at Old Hunter's feet – were too much for Lucky, and he crouched to leap down off the counter. He was brought up short, though, when Old Hunter stiffened and growled once more.

"No offence, Lucky," he rumbled threateningly, "but it took me long enough to find this stash. It's not for sharing, friend."

Lucky stared at him, his shoulders sagging. What was a friend, if not someone to share meat with? Indecisively he sat down on the counter once more. "But –"

"I've been guarding this since the Big Growl. You know how hard I've had to work to keep it? You're not the first dog to come along. And there were foxes."

Lucky licked the drool from his chops, his flanks shivering. He was almost unable to bear the closeness of food. The door of the big silver box behind Old Hunter hung off its hinges, and as well as the meat at the big dog's feet, there was more piled on the shelves. The metal box must have kept the meat cold, because he could see water pooling around the plastic-wrapped steaks, and some of them looked frozen solid – like the injured rabbit he'd found last winter. The meat might be frozen, but it would still be edible, even before it melted. He knew that. And there was so much of it …

"But there's plenty here …"

Old Hunter growled again, more angrily. "There's plenty of it, but it could be the last meat left to find. I can make it last. I *will* make it last, Lucky."

Lucky felt his whole body tense with the shock – this was so unlike his friend! Old Hunter had always been willing to share before, and for such a fierce-looking dog, he was known for being slow to anger. The Big Growl must have spooked Old Hunter very badly.

Lucky lay down, lowering his tail but not his head: he kept that proudly raised. "We've known each other a long time, Old Hunter. You've always shared with me."

"Things change, Lucky."

"*We* don't have to. We're both survivors. We always have been! You and I, we're tough. You're tougher than any dog I know."

The big dog stared at him, lips still tugged back from his teeth, but his suspicion was wavering. The tip of his tail twitched with indecision. Lucky saw it was flicking close to something else: something that dangled from a broken cold-box, dangerously close to the pooling meltwater of the frozen meat. For the first time in a long time, Lucky sensed the invisible power of the longpaws, prickling in his fur and blood.

"Old Hunter!" He lunged, banging his shoulder into the bigger dog's side. Old Hunter staggered sideways, away from the snaking thing, just as its severed tip brushed the pool of water and sparked viciously.

If Lucky hadn't taken him by surprise, he knew Old

Hunter would have fought him; as it was the big dog sprawled on his flank, staring in shock at the swinging, spitting cable.

"I'm sorry, Old Hunter, I –"

"No," he growled softly. "No, Lucky. Thank you. I should have known. Been more diligent. I thought the light-power was dead."

Cautiously regaining his feet, the old dog sniffed delicately at the water, then used a paw to swipe at the meat, knocking and dragging it safely away.

"Careful," said Lucky.

"I will be. The light-power snake would have bitten me. I'd be hurt or dead if you hadn't been here."

Now, decided Lucky, was a good time to stay silent.

"Know what?" Old Hunter said at last. "You're right, Lucky. The Big Growl's had everything its own way so far. Why should I let it beat me too?"

He took a pace back from his guarded meat.

Lucky yipped with relief and leapt down from the counter, giving a wide berth to the water and the power snake. He remembered his manners, licking Old Hunter's face with gratitude and affection, and the big dog reciprocated, making a far happier rumbling noise in his throat. Then, respect properly shown, they both began to wolf down the meat.

The half-frozen food tasted better than anything Lucky had ever eaten. He ate it quickly, noisily, messily. Only when he'd satisfied the worst of his hunger did he manage to slow down and gnaw at it more sociably with Old Hunter.

It was good to be eating with a friend.

"So," mumbled Old Hunter after a while, through a half-chewed bone. "Where were you when *It* happened?"

There was no need to ask what *It* was. "In the Trap House," said Lucky, shivering briefly at the awful memory. "They'd caught me a few no-suns before."

"Bad luck." Old Hunter shook his head.

"Not completely. The Big Growl freed me. Maybe the Earth-Dog took pity on me." He thought for a moment, becoming solemn. "I must remember to bury meat for her when I'm outside."

"A good idea. But leave enough for yourself. The Earth-Dog understands that."

"You're right." Lucky was grateful for Old Hunter's reassurance and his hard-earned wisdom. "And you? Where were you when it growled?"

The big dog grunted at a happier memory. "Hunting rabbits in the park. And catching them, I might add."

Lucky licked his jaws. Now that the hunger no longer chewed at his belly, he could remember the taste of fresh rabbit with pleasant nostalgia. "They're fun to chase," he remarked, "but hard to catch."

"You have to be wily," said the wise old dog, licking the last scraps of flesh off a bone. "Play friendly for a rabbit; make it think you're not a threat. Be calm and uninterested, however hungry you are. And then, when it's in paw range, pounce fast!"

"I've done that before, and it wriggled free."

"Let your whole weight fall on it. If you try and catch it with your paws, it'll squirm away and be gone before you know it."

"Thanks." All of Lucky's best hunting tips had always come from Old Hunter. "You must have been hunting in the wild since you were a pup! I really should practise proper hunting as well as scavenging and begging."

Old Hunter gnawed thoughtfully on the stripped bone, licking at the marrow. "I wasn't always in the wild," he murmured. He sat up and scratched at his neck with a hindleg, managing to part the fur a little. "See that?"

Lucky stared. The bare bit of skin, rubbed smooth and hairless, couldn't be what he thought it was. Could it?

"I spent time as a Leashed Dog."

Lucky couldn't believe it. "You lived with *longpaws*?"

"When I was no more than a pup," said Old Hunter

gruffly. "It didn't last long, thank goodness. They moved away and didn't bother to take me with them. That's when I started to survive on my own. But it's true: before then I was a Leashed Dog."

"What happened to it? The …" He found it difficult even to say the word.

"The collar? I took it off myself. It wasn't easy." Old Hunter's expression darkened. "I had no choice. I was growing, getting very big. It was cutting into my neck. Might have killed me in the end, but I chewed it off. Took me all day and half the night, but I did it. I swore I'd never wear another one."

A shudder rippled through Lucky's muscles. Collars were unnatural; dogs like him and Old Hunter should run free. That was the true way, the natural way.

What would a collar even feel like, locked around a dog's throat, choking and restricting? Maybe he knew. Something flickered in his memory. Was it possible …?

Very, very dimly Lucky could recall his old Pup-Pack. The other pups in it had worn collars, he was sure of it. So had he, too, worn one? A hated symbol of captivity, a sign of being in thrall to longpaws?

What had happened? Lucky wondered. What lay in his past that was so cloudy and elusive? He couldn't remember. More than that, he didn't *want* to remember;

and it wasn't just the fear of some perhaps-imaginary collar. Just thinking about the Pup-Pack made him feel sad, though he didn't know why. The memory brought with it other remembered sensations: warm bodies, small hearts beating close to his, the crush and comfort and noise of a crowded basket.

Lucky shook himself, unease lifting his fur. The half-forgotten images brought with them a horrible feeling: that dreadful cold sadness, like a stone in his belly. He got up on all fours, stretched away the dull pain. Dipping his head, he licked Old Hunter's ear.

"Thank you, friend."

"You're welcome, young one. Good luck to you."

Lucky hesitated. *Good luck* ... Didn't they both need more than that just now?

"Old Hunter ... I've been thinking. It might seem crazy, but why don't we team up for a while?" At the mute astonishment in his friend's eyes, he rushed on hurriedly. "Only for a little while, I mean. Only till we get used to – to all these changes."

Old Hunter still said nothing, only watched him a little sadly.

Not sure whether to take his silence as encouragement or not, Lucky rushed on. "I know we're both Lone Dogs at heart. I *know* that, and we belong on our own, in ordinary times. But everything's so strange and dangerous. The Big Growl has changed so much. Maybe it would be good to watch each other's backs for a little? We'd be a good team, you and I ..."

His voice trailed into silence. Old Hunter, too, stood up.

"I'm sorry, Lucky," he said gruffly. "It wouldn't do. It wouldn't feel ... right. It's like I said: we can't let the Big Growl win. We can't let it change *us*."

"But – the light-power snake. Remember how it nearly stung you? If we're together, we can –"

His friend's eyes grew harder. "You probably saved my life, that's true. But we have to keep on surviving alone, like we always have. Understand? It's every dog for himself."

Lucky bowed his head in reluctant agreement, and gave Old Hunter a last fond flick of his tongue. "I understand. But thank you again."

"Thank *you*. Here."

As he turned back, Old Hunter picked up a sizeable chunk of meat in his jaws and dropped it at Lucky's feet. Lucky pawed it, surprised.

"Go on, take it. I won't miss it."

Lucky gave him a grateful whine as he seized the meat in his jaws. He threw Old Hunter a last fond look as he leapt up on to the counter, then bounded back through the broken mall.

CHAPTER SEVEN

It wasn't long before he slowed to a gentle jog, then halted altogether. He shifted the meat in his mouth slightly. A full belly had made him sleepy, and here, close to where he'd entered the mall, he was standing in front of a very tempting bed.

This huge inner house held far bigger longpaw things than the others including a low, broad, squishy longpaw seat made of that same aged skin as the treas-ure-pouches. Lucky gazed at it with longing, and took a few paces towards it. He was so tired. He could rest, then eat when he woke, then move on again …

A pungent earthy musk assaulted his nostrils, overwhelming the enticing smell of his prospective bed.

Oh no …

There were animals around; he'd known that. Animal scavengers and longpaws, too. But he hadn't taken much notice when he'd cared only about finding food, when he'd had nothing they could take from him.

Now he did.

Lucky tightened his grip on the chunk of flesh, growling softly. There was a high stack of wooden shelves behind the seat, and he sensed something hidden there. A sharp black nose twitched, followed by mean predatory eyes and huge pricked ears. Lucky's growl became louder, more threatening, as the grey fox eyed him.

Then, around the shelving, three more of them padded, thin and vicious-looking. They exchanged glances.

Their Alpha's yellow eyes glinted, and they stalked forward with arrogant snarls.

"Meat, dog. Give us *now!*"

Still gripping the hunk, snarling deep in his throat, Lucky sized up his enemy. Each fox was maybe half his size, but there were four of them and their eyes were sharp. A desperate fox was a dangerous creature – especially one in a Pack. As he watched them, all four crept forward, showing their fangs.

They were confident, he realised, and clever – dividing themselves into pairs on either flank. A cold knot of fear formed in his stomach. They were going to attack from two directions, and Lucky knew he stood little chance of fighting them off. He could drop the meat. Drop the meat, and run –

No!

He couldn't lose this food. He had no idea when he'd find more – and besides, they were *foxes!* He was a dog, and a tough Lone Dog at that – no scrawny fox was going to take what was his.

His eyes darted from side to side as he watched the foxes manoeuvre, slinking under small tables and edging around obstacles. They were forming a circle now, closing in, and Lucky felt a prickle of terror at his raised hackles.

"Silly dog, stupid dog," hissed the Alpha, his voice thick and distorted.

Another joined in. "No friends! No help! Ha!"

"Wish you stayed with *big* dog, *scary* dog," smirked a third. "Silly dog!"

He'd eaten, he reminded himself, and would have more stamina than these desperate creatures. What was more, hadn't he escaped the Big Growl? Hadn't he already dodged raccoons and sharpclaws and an angry Fierce Dog?

I can get out of this!

Lucky focused on the Alpha before him. Curling back his lips around the meat, he glared and growled. The other animal gave him a cocky grin.

Without warning, Lucky charged forward, straight into the Alpha. The fox gave an astonished yelp as he knocked it flying into a broken longpaw sitting box. Lucky kicked his back paws into its belly, and it gave a yelp of pain, winded. Lucky didn't waste a moment. He fled, bolting though the mall as fast as he could.

Lucky heard the leader scramble back to its feet, recovering fast. The rest were already screeching at his heels, snarling and squealing with rage and frustration. Lucky was fast, but desperate hunger was giving them an edge, and he was hampered by the meat in his jaws, hardly able to draw breath. He nipped between pillars and raced through the open area where longpaws used to sit and eat, crashing over tables and sitting boxes. He skidded through water that leaked from a place he couldn't see, but the foxes wouldn't be shaken.

A rack of longpaw furs went flying; then Lucky was back on the metal hill and fleeing down, his claws scrabbling wildly as he tried not to fall head over hindpaws. At the bottom of the metal hill another big longpaw seat loomed, and he leapt.

No! Mid-leap, the chunk of meat slipped from his

panting jaws. He caught sight of it, slithering beneath a broad wooden table, with a loose blue fur hanging over it.

Lucky doubled back and skidded after it, the soft blue fur falling back to conceal him.

His flanks heaving, Lucky pricked his ears and panted as silently as he could. He could smell the foxes, sharp and earthy and coming closer. If they heard him, or smelled him – and he knew his panic and fear must be strong-scented – he was as good as dead.

He heard a low snarling and snuffling as they searched the air with sharp noses. They muttered to themselves and each other. Some of it was incomprehensible; some of it all too clear.

"Dog close," growled one. He spat the word *dog* with disgust in his rasping high fox-voice.

"*Meat* close," said another, and there was huffing, hungry fox-laughter.

Lucky wrinkled his muzzle. To think these scrawny scavengers were his cousin-kind!

He knew he didn't have long before they found him. Fear rippled down his spine, raising his fur. He had to force himself not to whine in terror. There was a fox at each side of the table.

"Noise! There!" yipped one suddenly. "Go see!

Is dog?"

Heart thundering, Lucky strained to hear the clicking paws as they moved slowly, so slowly, away from his table. Any second now, they'd realise the noise was a false alarm – a rat, or a bird – and then they'd be back …

Seizing the meat, he bolted, heading straight for the centre of the mall. They were squealing behind him once more, giving chase, but at least he'd escaped the trap of that table. Lucky pounded on, pain jabbing sharply at his wounded paw, his lungs aching, his whole body feeling heavy and awkward now. He felt the first wrench of despair in his gut. The foxes were going to get him.

Close to the entrance the displays of longpaw treasure seemed more cluttered. No longpaw thief or scavenging dog had bothered to take the brightly-coloured beads and bottles. A whole rack of them crashed to the ground as Lucky slammed sideways into it, then veered around another high counter and leapt over a broken shelf. At least all the clutter was holding up the foxes too; he could hear them stumbling and skidding behind him.

A rack of small bottles went tumbling and shattering, sending sickeningly powerful scents to assault his nose. *High ground,* he thought. *I should find high ground.* Somewhere to make a stand, somewhere to stay safe …

There. Lucky leapt on to a tall counter, scattering paper and strange metal machines, the biggest of which fell to the floor. It exploded open, paper and small metal discs scattering everywhere, and Lucky nearly followed it, sliding helplessly on the smooth surface. Scrabbling, he finally came to a stop on the counter, and sprang to his feet.

Panting hard, he stared down at the circling, grinning foxes.

"Can't stay up," came one menacing growl. "No, can't, silly dog. Not forever."

"Must come down!" said one of them.

"Soon, boys. Soon." The hissing snarl was confident enough to send a thrill of fear through Lucky's shivering flanks.

They were right, he realised. He *couldn't* stay up here forever. He could take another flying leap, of course, over their heads and away, but the terrible pain in his paw had finally overcome the thrill of the chase. The stabbing of the wound was a pure white agony that almost made him dizzy.

Lucky's flanks rose and fell swiftly with his desperate breath. Had this really been worth it, for one chunk of meat?

The answer came straight from his wild instinct: a

fury that raced through him, humming in his limbs and flanks, his muscles preparing for a last fight. *Of course it was worth it.*

He was bigger and better than these foxes. Submit to these creatures, and he was unworthy of being a dog.

Besides, in the new world after the Big Growl, it wasn't cowards who would survive. It was the brave, and the strong, and the determined. And he *would not* give up his rightful prey!

He laid the meat between his forepaws, prepared to guard it to the death – just as Old Hunter would. Lowering his head, raising his hackles high and baring his teeth in a lethal snarl, he summoned all his energy for one last, wild bark of rage and defiance.

And then he hesitated.

The strange noise seemed to come from nowhere. It certainly didn't come from him, or the foxes. And yet it was there, swelling to fill the echoing hall.

A low, menacing growl.

Suddenly nervous, the foxes twitched their heads from side to side, ears pricked. In an instant, all four had sprung round to face the shattered entrance.

Scarcely able to believe what he was seeing, Lucky stared at the group that was approaching. *Dogs – more dogs!*

A little crossbreed, short-legged and hairy-faced, her pink tongue poking out in excitement. A sleek black-and-white Farm Dog, clutching a huge leather item in his mouth. A snub-faced, short-legged, ugly brute of a Fight Dog, whose eyes were full of hectic fear. A small thing, with long white hair. And a giant, furry black dog with a broad head and determined eyes.

They barely gave Lucky a glance, all their nervous attention focused on the foxes. They were such a strange Pack. Then the last dog entered. She was handsome and long-legged, with gold-and-white fur. In fact, she reminded Lucky of his own reflection, before the city's clear-stone shattered. And there was something about her scent …

But there was no time to wonder any more. The newcomers were facing up to the foxes, who formed a ragged line and snarled back in insolent defiance.

"A gang – very scary!" The smallest fox sneered at the lineup.

The Alpha laughed, a cackling yelp of derision. "Scary? You *think?*"

Lucky felt his shoulders start to droop. He'd been glad to see more dogs approaching, but now that he'd had a closer look … maybe the foxes were right to laugh. At least they had some sort of battle formation. The new arrivals looked more like puppies let loose without a Mother-Dog. The little crossbreed might have been brave for her size, but she seemed incapable of doing anything other than run in excited circles. The long-haired pretty one was yapping hysterically. The ugly Fight Dog was doing his best to attack the foxes, but the big black giant was getting hopelessly in the way.

It was the dog who looked like Lucky, the handsome-faced golden dog, who kept her nerve, charging straight for the foxes. Behind her raced the Fight Dog, dodging the black giant at last, and the Farm Dog, who at least had dropped his piece of padded leather.

The skirmish was brief and vicious. Teeth snapped and claws raked; from his position Lucky saw the Fight Dog grab for a fox's leg and almost instantly lose it – but not before he'd drawn blood, and the fox had yipped in shock and pain. The leader-fox sprang at the black-and-white Farm Dog, jaws slavering, but the golden dog spun with surprising agility and raked its scabby grey flank with her teeth, knocking it off balance. Even the pretty little longhair was standing her ground, barking furiously, though she flinched at an attack; the big black dog pounced to protect her flank, sending a fox tumbling across the slick floor. A paw lashed out, drawing blood from a fox's muzzle, and its head snapped sideways, trailing a sliver of drool.

The foxes had a wiry ferocity, and they were willing to fight, but they were too smart to stand up for long to a Pack of dogs, however chaotic. When it became clear they were outnumbered and outsized, the Alpha fox gave a high and vicious bark.

"Go, boys! No point!"

With a final vicious snap and snarl, the last fox turned tail and bolted after its escaping companions.

"Brave in a Pack!" it sniggered, making a mocking face at Lucky as it scampered away. "Coward dogs!"

As they vanished into the chaos of the mall, Lucky breathed easily for the first time since he'd left Old Hunter behind. Thrashing his tail in wild gratitude, he gave the newcomers a brief friendly bark.

"Thanks. You saved my hide!"

Panting, they all turned to look up at him in renewed anxiety, as if they'd only just remembered he was there. The Fight Dog took a couple of paces towards him and sniffed. Although his body looked hard with muscle, his stance was nervous.

"You're welcome," he rumbled gruffly. "Foxes! Hah!"

"I thought I was done for." The flood of relief made Lucky almost weak with gratitude to this motley Pack.

"Happy to help!" yipped the crossbreed, almost falling over her own feet as she spun.

The dog that looked like Lucky said nothing at first. She leapt up on to the counter, and though Lucky moved instinctively to protect his food, she ignored the meat altogether. Instead, she sniffed hesitantly at him. Their eyes met, and Lucky's heart leapt inside his chest.

Something in his gut tugged at him, stirring sense-memories, sparking images in his head. He knew this dog…

She blinked her dark friendly eyes, and nuzzled his face.

"It's really you!" she barked softly. "Dear Yap, it's *you!* Hello, my brother!"

CHAPTER EIGHT

Yap ...!

A pang of memory twisted inside Lucky, and the heavy stone-feeling of loneliness in his belly lifted just a little. *Yap!* How long had it been since he'd heard his Pup name? And hers came back to him in a tumble of sounds and images. A snuffling nose, an insistent squeaking, a body nestled close to his, tiny paws shoving him, golden skin and fur pressed cosily against his own ... and yes, again and always, that constant talkative squealing ...

"Squeak! It's you!" Overcome by happiness, he licked at her face, and she crouched playfully on her forepaws to nibble at his throat.

"I'm not Squeak any more," she yipped. "I have a

new name. Bella!"

"Bella," Lucky repeated, getting used to the sound. "That's beautiful," he decided.

There was a snorting yelp from the pretty white dog, and a *shut up!* growl as the crossbreed beside her nipped her nose. Lucky realised the whole motley Pack was sitting there, ogling him and his new-found litter-sister. They looked both fascinated and expectant, though the Fight Dog had a defensive expression. They might be an odd assortment of dogs, but they all looked very fine in their own way. Their fur was sleek, their bellies round, their muzzles free of fleabites and scratches, except for the few scrapes the foxes had managed to inflict before they ran. Poised on three legs, one forepaw delicately raised, the pretty dog might have had her long glossy hair brushed by a longpaw just that sun-up.

Despite her pert confidence, though, she seemed a little ashamed of her outburst, and Bella was giving her a stern glance of disapproval. "My name means, *Sunshine.* Bella means *beautiful.*"

Lucky nudged Bella's muzzle with his own, as much to calm her down as show affection. "I have a new name, too," he told her. "I'm *Lucky.*"

She washed his ear with her tongue. "The name fits! You're certainly lucky we came along just now!"

"You're right about that." Lucky stepped back, and studied Bella's friends. "Hello," he said.

Sunshine seemed too intimidated to reply, and quite off-balance with her paw in the air. The Fight Dog grunted some inaudible answer, but he was standing up on his hindpaws and sniffing hungrily at the meat Lucky had left on the counter.

"Oh, Bruno." Bella gave him a playful growl and a nudge with her muzzle. "You're always hungry. Even at the end of the world, you're thinking of food."

Don't all dogs think of food and how to get it? The end of the world wasn't a joke – it was real, he thought, remembering the terror of the Big Growl, the horrible endless depths of the crevice in the road. Getting and keeping food *wasn't* a joke. He knew that. But perhaps these sleek, well-fed dogs didn't.

As if to prove him right, Sunshine flopped on to her plump belly, her white coat spreading on the ground. She gave a whine. "I wish you wouldn't say those things, Bella. We don't *know* the world's ended."

Bella's answering whine held a touch of irritation, though she licked reassuringly at the black button nose. "If the world hasn't ended, Sunshine, where do you suppose our longpaws are?"

Lucky stiffened. *Our* longpaws? In disbelief he

studied each dog, all so very different, except for one thing. Every single one of them wore the ownership sign of the longpaws.

Horrified, he couldn't help exclaiming out loud.

"You're *Leashed Dogs!*"

They all stared at him, and then at each other, bemused.

"Yes?" said the Farm Dog, cocking his head curiously.

"It – well, that explains – I mean, the way you all –" Lucky fell silent, his mind a turmoil. *Leashed* Dogs. *Pampered* Dogs. Tame, silly, *pointless* Dogs ...

They'd let longpaws buckle collars round their necks. They relied on longpaws for food, for fun, for exercise, for a place to sleep. Without their longpaws they were helpless, hopeless ... the horror of it was beyond belief. How were *Leashed* Dogs supposed to survive the end of the world?

Lucky shook himself free of the shivers in his fur. He couldn't think about it just now. Besides, what did it matter at this moment, when they'd come to his rescue with such good timing?

Lucky glanced back at Bruno, still snuffling at the meat with his ugly blunt muzzle. "Come on. Let's share this." He leapt up on to the counter and grabbed it in his jaws, then jumped back down and dropped it. "You saved me *and* this meat. I owe you a share. It's the least I can do."

And it's all you'll get if you can't hunt by yourselves …

For a while there was only the contented sound of tearing and chewing as the odd little Pack shared Lucky's spoils. Wolfing down his own portion, Lucky murmured to Bella, "Your friends are … interesting."

Bella lifted her head and gazed at them fondly. "They're not like us at all, are they? I used to think all dogs were Sheltie-Retrievers!"

Lucky blinked. "Is that what we are?"

"Yes. Don't you remember our Sire and Mother-Dog?" Her expression was filled with conflicted emotion – relief, deep happiness, regret at their long separation – but there was amusement in her voice, too. "Most of us have proper kind-names, names the longpaws gave to all of us."

Lucky grunted disapprovingly. "Things aren't *proper* just because the longpaws invented them."

Bella ignored that. "Now, Bruno there, he's a 'bulldog'. And Mickey's what the longpaws call a "Border Collie'. He's very smart, likes to herd us! Daisy's Sire and Mother-Dog were a 'Westie' and a 'Jack Russell'. Little Sunshine, there – she's a 'Maltese'. *Very* delicate," she added.

"And this one?" Lucky nodded at the huge black dog.

"Martha? She's a 'Newfoundland'. Look at the size of her next to Sunshine!"

Lucky eyed the pair. Martha was much taller than Lucky, and Sunshine didn't even reach up as far as her knee joint. The foxes had been right about one thing: this really was the most unorganised Pack he'd ever laid eyes on. Were they even a real Pack at all? Who was their Alpha? Bella talked a lot, and she was kind but brusque with Sunshine, but she didn't act like a Pack leader. She didn't have that air of unquestioned authority; she didn't expect to be obeyed at her first bark or nip, and even when she seemed decisive, she looked to the others for approval or advice. The collie-dog, Mickey, seemed intelligent, and Bruno the bulldog looked like he could handle himself in a fight, but neither of them had played the Alpha with the foxes. Sunshine – certainly not! And Daisy seemed brave, and scrappy, and feisty, but she was barely out of puppyhood, no Alpha dog either …

Who was in *charge* of this Pack?

Lucky's bewildered thoughts were interrupted by a high panicked howl. Sunshine had leapt up, abandoning her last delicate morsel of meat, and was running in tight circles, long hair floating, claws skittering in panic.

"I'm hurt! I'm hurt!"

"What –" began Bella.

"The foxes! *I got bitten!*" Sunshine's yelping was becoming hysterical, and she lifted one paw pathetically off the ground. It was the forepaw she'd been favouring since the fight, and now Lucky realised there was a reason – one she'd only just discovered herself. Waving her paw in the air, flapping it though she was still trying to run, Sunshine instantly fell over. She got up on three paws, still panicking, and flew in circles again.

"My longpaw! I need my longpaw *now! I need to go to the vet!*"

Lucky saw that Bella looked anxious, her eyes wide. He was taken aback by a sudden scornful disdain. No, his sister *really* wasn't an Alpha dog.

But the others were no better. Mickey had sprung to his feet, staring. Daisy was yapping wildly in sympathy, and suddenly the others joined in.

"We'll go back to the longpaw houses!"

"No, we can find a vet! Find a vet!"

"Where? Where will we find a vet? They're ALL GONE!"

"The *longpaws* are all gone! What will we *do?*"

Snapping out of his disbelief, Lucky jumped to his feet and gave a single angry bark.

"Calm *down!*"

Falling silent, they stared at him. He thought back to the longpaw he'd seen with the vivid yellow coat. Should he tell the dogs about his encounter? But that longpaw had been so ... strange. No, it would only confuse matters – make them think there was a longpaw around to help.

He stood straighter. "I don't know what a *vet* is, but I'm sure Sunshine doesn't need one. Let me see."

Tentatively, her flanks quivering, Sunshine crept forward and shyly offered him her paw. Lucky sniffed at it. There was a smear of blood, sure enough, but it was no more than a tiny tear in the skin. He touched it delicately with his tongue.

"Here, it's just a scratch. That's all. I'll show you." Lying down, Lucky stretched out his own wounded paw, turning the pad up for their examination, and there was a collective gasp of horror.

"That's terrible!" squeaked Sunshine. "You need a vet more than I do!"

"No I don't," said Lucky in exasperation. "It's only bad because I haven't stopped long enough to tend to it. Look." He licked carefully at the wound. Sure enough, it felt better already. *Maybe if I had given it more attention before, I would have had an easier time getting away from those foxes,* he thought. He licked at it again. "Come on, Sunshine. Try it."

Obediently Sunshine bent her head and licked rather dubiously at the scratch on her own paw. When nothing terrible happened, she tried again, and was soon washing it quite painstakingly.

"You're right," she whispered in awe. "It doesn't sting as much. It *does* feel better." She stopped licking to gaze admiringly at Lucky. "He's right, everybody!"

"You see?" he barked. "You don't need a silly longpaw vet!"

They were all staring at him in respectful silence. He met their eyes, feeling a ripple of unease in his fur.

"That's wonderful," murmured Martha, lowering her big black head and tilting it to study Sunshine's paw.

"Fine job. Fine job!" growled Bruno. "Splendid!"

"You're so *clever!*" exclaimed little Daisy. "I can't believe you knew that!"

Mickey said nothing, but he looked profoundly impressed. Even Bella was gazing from him to Sunshine and back again, with delight. Six tails wagged and thumped.

Oh no, you don't! thought Lucky. *I'm not your Alpha!*

Hastily he rose again, and backed off a step. "Listen, I – I'm really grateful you helped me out there. You were the best!" He retreated another couple of paces, his hackles rising. "But I've got to go. Thank you, again. And good luck!"

Before any of them could react, he had turned and was trotting as fast as he could out of the mall. He could feel their stunned gazes, could almost sense those drooping tails and ears, but he wouldn't look back. Would *not* look back—

Lucky came to a halt. Beyond the empty windows of the wrecked store, the sky had turned a dark charcoal grey, heavy with water. Even as he hesitantly lifted a paw to step outside, brilliant light lit the street for a fraction of an instant, and then a colossal bang shook the world.

Lucky froze.

Lightning!

In a second there would be battering water, falling in torrents from the sky. The shattering crash of a terrible war in the clouds, where the Sky-Dogs fought to the death over and over again, and Lightning the Swift Dog hero teased the Earth-Dog by tearing through the sky leaving fire in his wake. There was very little that frightened Lucky, but he hated to be outside when the sky burst its clouds …

He'd hesitated too long, and he could feel Bella's warmth, her flanks close against his. She didn't look at him, but watched the warring black skies too.

"Stay with us, Lucky," she said at last. "Just for

a while?"

For a long moment he couldn't answer. He thought about the loneliness he'd felt when he woke this sun-up, and the empty realisation that Sweet was no longer there. He remembered the warmth and tumble of the Pup-Pack, the smell of Squeak cuddling up beside him as they slept. And now Squeak was Bella, and she was beside him again, different but the same …

"Okay," he said at last, slowly. "Just for a little while, though."

She gave a loud bark of delight, and suddenly she was down on her forepaws, then leaping up, tumbling into him. Unexpected joy fizzed through Lucky's body and he rolled with her, jumping up and spinning in a circle, then letting her chase him back towards the little Pack.

The others looked thrilled. Daisy darted forward, yapping and colliding with Bella, and solid old Bruno knocked the little dog playfully sideways so that she and Sunshine fell in a heap. Then they were all chasing and barking and play-fighting, as if they didn't have a care in the world.

An empty longpaw mall was the best place in the world for a game, Lucky decided as he dodged Martha's lumbering pounce. Mickey dropped his precious leather item to grab a fallen longpaw fur, shaking it like a rat, and then Bruno had seized it too and the collie and the bulldog were rolling around in a chaotic tug-of-war.

Lucky watched happily until he felt Bella cannon into him and the two dogs wrestled in a squirming heap.

"Are you all right?" panted Bella breathlessly.

"Of course! Come on!" Lucky sprang for her again.

Even Sunshine joined in, yelping wildly and spinning, trying hopelessly to jump on Martha and knock her over. Chasing Mickey in circles, Lucky spotted piles of the metal pots the Food House longpaw cooked with. He'd always liked the noise of those! Lucky plunged into the middle of the stacks, and the pots went flying with a most satisfying, deafening racket.

At last, exhausted, the dogs lay down panting one by one. Sunshine had found a pile of silk cushions; Mickey lay contentedly beside her. Lucky stretched out on the cold, hard floor, watching them all. As Daisy flopped beside him, he gave her ear an affectionate lick.

"Lucky, come up here!" Bella's head hung over the edge of a big longpaw seat, her ears pricked.

Uncertainly, he rose and put first one paw, then the other, against its soft cowhide body. He sprang on to it, and curled up beside Bella, who gave a happy little whine and licked his nose.

Lucky closed his eyes, tilting his head up to wish for a good sleep. *Moon-Dog, watch over us …*

"What are you doing?" Bella's surprised voice broke into his reverie.

"What am I –?" Lucky paused, dumbfounded. "I'm getting ready to sleep …"

"You are ready to sleep." She stared at him as he turned three times.

Lucky stopped turning and cocked his head at her curiously. Didn't Bella prepare for rest properly? He lowered his head, sniffing dubiously at the sofa, then met her eyes.

"Stop fidgeting, Lucky," she said softly.

"I can't help it." He shifted position, trying to settle. "This is just too comfy …"

"No such thing," she yawned. "You'll get used to it quickly, believe me!"

Lucky thought about that for a few moments. "You must have been happy with your longpaws," he said softly.

"I was …"

"Where are they now? What happened, Bella?"

"Oh." She laid her head on her forepaws, lifting her ears as if hearing something in her memory. She sighed. "It was such a rush, when the Big Growl came. Such a terrible panic. They left in a great hurry. Piled all their possessions into their loudcage, and drove away. All their possessions," she murmured sadly, "except me."

Well, what did she expect? They were longpaws, weren't they? She shouldn't have relied on them, shouldn't have built her happiness on a Leashed life … but Lucky nuzzled his sister's head and licked at her ear. "I'm sorry, Bella."

"That's all right, Lucky. I don't miss them. Not much, anyway. I can't be that sad – they left me behind, after all. *They* abandoned *me*." There was bitterness in her voice, but she shook herself.

Now you're beginning to understand, thought Lucky. He was sorry she'd been hurt, but the sooner she hardened herself against her old life, the happier she'd be. There was hope for her.

"Besides," she went on, "I have other things to think about. My friends, for a start. They need someone to take charge. I don't have time to mope."

"Good for you," said Lucky, glad his litter-sister was so practical and unsentimental. Just like him, in fact. She'd make a good Free Dog …

"But what happened to you, Lucky?"

"What do you mean?"

"After the Pup-Pack."

"Oh …" Lucky closed his eyes. What was the point in dragging up those memories? They weren't happy ones. Still, Bella was his sister. He could tell her. If he could recall it …

The memories were hazy and half-blurred, like looking into a pond for small prey that kept dodging out of view. But slowly, haltingly, they began to take shape.

"I remember them taking me … the longpaws. They smiled, looked happy … oh! I didn't wriggle." He raised the muscles above his eyes, surprised. "I didn't try to get free. That's so strange. Why didn't I run away?"

"We didn't," said Bella. "Not then. Not as pups. Go on."

"I remember the longpaws' house." Beyond the broken clear-stone at the mall entrance, the Sky-Dogs' fire lit the world for an instant, followed by the crash of thunder as the battle resumed. The dreadful sound echoed the unhappiness of Lucky's memories, and a shudder ran through his flanks. "The longpaws didn't smile so much, there, in their home. There were small longpaws, like pups. They never left me alone. Chasing me, picking me up, teasing me. I remember being so tired, just wanting to be left alone …"

"Longpaw pups are like that," nodded Bella. "But they're not so bad once they get used to you."

"No, but the big longpaw was. He was strange. Sometimes he toppled over, like an old tree, and he smelled so wrong. Like the longpaw fire-juice, but stale. When he smelled very badly of it, he couldn't stay on his legs. And he would get so angry. I remember ..." Lucky closed his eyes more tightly, not liking the effort of recollection. "I remember his paws more than anything. Kicking out at me. Sometimes getting me. He shouted and kicked and was always angry, even when he didn't smell of that fire-juice."

Bella nuzzled him. "Your longpaws don't sound like mine at all."

"Some longpaws are good, that's true." Lucky thought of the Food House longpaw with a twinge of sadness. "But not this one. All I wanted to do was get away from him. He scared me. One day the door was open – by mistake I think – and I made a run for it. I ran and ran and ..."

"And?"

"And I never went back." He sighed, relieved the story was over. "Things have been good for me ever since then. I've been happy on my own, and I've learnt to take care of myself. I don't have to be scared of anyone any more, and I never will be, ever again."

Bella nestled closer against him.

"Do you remember the stories our Mother-Dog used to tell us when we were pups?" she asked.

"Of course," said Lucky, thinking of the flash of lightning he'd just seen.

"I'm thinking about the story of Omega Wind and the Forest-Dog. Do you remember it?"

Lucky frowned. "Not completely," he said. He licked his litter-sister's ear affectionately. "How did it go?"

"Well, there was once a little dog called Wind who was the least important dog in her Pack. They called her Omega and made her fetch and carry for them and do everything they said. The Alpha of the Pack was a cruel Fierce Dog who always bit Wind whenever she was too slow in carrying out his orders.

"But Wind dreamed of leaving the Pack and being free from all her duties, and she used to sneak into the forest and hunt small creatures by herself. Omega dogs were forbidden to hunt, so she always ate half of her prey and left the rest as a tribute to the Forest-Dog.

"Then the Storm of Dogs arrived, the world turned upside down. Wind's Pack were one of the first to be attacked by the giant dogs who came down from the mountains. Wind ran away into the forest, with one of the giant dogs on her heels, and she thought she would be caught and torn to shreds.

"But the Forest-Dog had been watching Wind since she started to leave him her tribute, and he loved her because she was cunning and she wouldn't give up, just as the Sky-Dogs loved Lightning for his speed. So the Forest-Dog helped her to climb into a tree so that the giant dogs couldn't find her, and she was saved from the carnage of the Storm of Dogs.

"From that day on, Wind was a Lone Dog, going wherever she pleased and never obeying any Alpha dog's command again. You'll never see her, but sometimes when you're in the deep forest you can hear her, howling in the trees with her friend the Forest-Dog."

Bella nuzzled Lucky. "You remind me of that story," she said. "You escaped, and it made you a strong, free Lone Dog. I'm just sorry your longpaw Alpha was so cruel."

Lucky laid his head down beside Bella's. Of course he didn't need the sympathy she was offering him, but just lying next to her again, after all this time, felt reassuring. The fear and the loneliness of this sun-up seemed very distant with his litter-sister here. Huddled against her warm side, listening to her tell one of their Mother-Dog's stories, it was as if something unlocked in his mind. The happy times flooded back into his head as he thought of his days with the Pup-Pack, that misty muddle of sensations: safety and affection and fullness in his belly. And companionship …

They had been good days. But that was a long time ago, Lucky reminded himself. The company of other little dogs was natural for a puppy – as natural as needing his Mother-Dog beside him, looking after him and loving him. But he wasn't a puppy any more. He was a grown dog, a Lone Dog.

Lucky didn't think he'd ever be able to sleep on this too-comfortable longpaw seat, and he lay for a while listening to the snores of Bruno, the small dream-whimpers of Sunshine and Daisy, the low soft breathing of Bella beside him. All the same he must have dozed off, because the next thing he was aware of was shafts of late sunlight reaching into the broken mall, making the other dogs stir and stretch and whine.

The roar and clash of the Sky-Dog battle in the sky had ceased altogether, and water no longer battered down. From outside came the beautiful scent of a fresh new day, washed clean by the cloudwater. Bella raised her head as Lucky got to his feet and stretched his forepaws.

"The Sky-Dogs have destroyed the clouds," he mused. "That's good."

"It's *very* good," cried Daisy. "Time to go home!"

"Yes!" yipped Sunshine. "Come on, then. Let's go!"

"Wait a minute." Lucky looked at them all, perplexed. "Home? Where's home?"

"Where we come from, of course!" Bella licked his face.

"Come with us!" Sunshine jumped up against his flanks, panting with adoration.

"Our longpaws are gone," said Martha mournfully. "But our homes are still there."

Bruno nodded sagely. "They're quite right, Lucky. Shame to be on your own. You're tough, I dare say, but even you probably need someone to watch your back now and then." The dog flexed his muscles and leaned forward on his broad stocky forelegs. "Bit of a fighter myself, you know? Handy in a tight corner, if I say so myself. How about it, hm?"

In their varying ways they all had that pleading look. Bruno was trying not to look too keen, but he wasn't hiding it well. Mickey, his precious belonging still in his jaws, was gazing at him with beseeching eyes, as was Martha. As for the two smaller dogs, they were jumping up and down at him till Lucky felt like swatting them with a paw.

He sighed, and glanced at Bella. She too was looking at him with a combination of kindness and fervent hope, and he remembered how good it had felt, waking up at her side.

Old Hunter was right – the Big Growl didn't have to change them – but perhaps Lone Dogs could make temporary concessions in a strange new world. There would be no longpaws in this "home" they talked about, but there might be a few comforts. The decision was simple, when he thought of it like that.

"Yes, all right," he said. "I'll come with you. For now!"

Bella yipped, dancing with delight, and the others gave in to a volley of happy barks, Daisy spinning on her hindpaws till she fell over. Lucky watched them, flattered that he was the source of such excitement.

Lucky still wasn't a Pack Dog, and he never would be. But who in their right mind would call *this* a proper Pack?

CHAPTER NINE

"Oh, we were friends long before the Big Growl," explained Bruno as he muscled his way to Lucky's side. "Isn't that right, everyone?"

They'd left the mall far behind now, and Lucky was conscious that the territory was growing far less familiar. He'd usually haunted the bustling parts of the city where scraps were plentiful – as were hiding places. Now the views were opening up, and the streets grew broader and leafier. Remembering the longpaw's fire-box yesterday, and the Fierce Dog who'd guarded it, Lucky's senses bristled with alertness.

The shadows were lengthening again, and the ruins of high buildings were haloed in brilliant light. Fountains of water still gushed from broken pipes, the droplets glittering prettily, and around him Lucky recognised the kind of once-neat houses where longpaws lived and slept. Uneasily, he wondered when those longpaws would return – and whether they ever would. Surely they'd come back for their lost companions? He knew longpaws didn't like to leave their friends to dissolve naturally into the earth, that they liked to bury them as if they were preserving precious bones. So why hadn't they returned yet?

But Lucky didn't have time to brood and wonder. The other dogs chatted constantly, vying for his attention, and once or twice he almost tripped over little Daisy as she scuttled in front of him.

"That's right!" she exclaimed now, and Lucky shortened his steps to avoid standing on her. "We've been friends for ages. We all live on the same street."

"And play in the same dog parks!" added Mickey. "Do you think the sandpit's still there, Bella?"

"I don't see what harm could come to the sandpit," observed Martha. "One day our longpaws will be back, and we'll all go there again. Maybe Lucky could come too!" She gave him a hopeful glance.

A *sandpit?* Lucky tried not to let his muzzle curl. Perhaps these dogs had never grown out of their Pup-

Pack days. He ignored Martha's expectant eyes for the moment. "So you're … friends. And so are your –" he hesitated, confused by the unfamiliar notion "– so are your longpaws. But, it's not like – well, it's not *exactly* like being in a Pack, is it?"

"No!" Sunshine shuddered. "Not like a *wild* Pack."

"Although it *was* a sort of a Pack," mused Bella. "We played together, and sometimes ate together, and we all knew each other."

There's more to being in a Pack than that, thought Lucky.

"And our longpaws – they were in a kind of Pack of their own," added Mickey. "They were always together too. That's why it was so much fun." His eyes grew wistful.

"It'll be fun again, just you wait!" yelped Sunshine. "My longpaw will be back for me, I know she will. She'll come back for the Frisbee-throw – she *always* took that with her – and she'll come back for me."

Lucky caught Bella's eye. He didn't want to say anything to spoil Sunshine's moment of optimistic joy, and he was relieved that Bella too said nothing. But his litter-sister's eyes were sad, and her ears drooped a little. She at least was beginning to understand how much had changed. If only they'd *all* listen to what the Earth-Dog was telling them. If only they knew how to tune their senses into the world. Perhaps that instinct was lost to them?

He nuzzled Bella's face, sure that no one else would have noticed her fleeting expression of foreboding. After all, the dogs were all licking one another's faces now, cheerfully wishing one another farewell and happy dreams …

What? Lucky stared around at them as they bid him goodnight and set off in different directions, each dog trotting happily into a different longpaw house. What in the name of the Sky-Dogs were they doing? They knew nothing of Pack rules – like staying together, like obeying the Alpha, like watching each other's backs … Lucky had never in his life felt such an expert on Pack life.

And it wasn't only the splitting of the Pack that worried him. Here on this street the longpaw homes were still standing, but only just. Some of the walls had vicious wounds where the Big Growl had snapped at them. Many of the windows were broken, and water escaped beneath doors, collecting into a growing pool in the middle of the road. There was a smell of longpaw waste, too, from beneath the ground, but the strongest scent in Lucky's nostrils was the scent of danger.

"Are you sure you should sleep here?" Lucky paused

behind Bella, bringing her to a quizzical halt.

"What? Oh, it's safe now, Lucky. Don't worry. The Big Growl's faded away."

"It could come back," he reminded her. "Some of these longpaw homes are damaged. Look at that wall – it's leaning. And those things wriggling out of the wall like snakes – don't you feel the invisible power? Can't you hear it singing?" He shivered, remembering how close Old Hunter had come to being struck down. Lucky didn't want to have to rescue anyone else from the brutal force. "There's still danger here, Bella. And who knows if the Big Growl will leave us alone?"

"Oh, Lucky." Bella licked his face affectionately. "No wonder you're nervous, after what happened in the Trap House. But these are our *homes*. Real, proper longpaw houses."

"I don't know." His hackles were still bristling. "I think we should sleep outside. And why are you all going into different houses? I may not know much about Packs, but isn't the whole point that you stay together? Then you keep each other warm at night, and protect each other."

Bella glanced back at the others, confused. "But Lucky, these are our homes. We have to be here when our longpaws come back. Don't you see how important that is?"

No, thought Lucky. *No, I really don't.* But he couldn't
say so to Bella – and besides, there was a determined
gleam in her eye that he couldn't help respecting. He
knew he'd end up helping her, going with her into the
longpaw house. It was the least he could do for his litter-
sister.

When he padded inside the longpaw house, Lucky
could understand Bella's reluctance to stay outside.
It was true that some of the longpaws' belongings had
been tipped over and smashed, and there were ominous
wounds in the walls, running from floor to ceiling. But
mostly the rooms were dry, and there was no doubt it was
a more comfortable place to be than the road outside.

For a Leashed Dog, he reminded himself.

As he padded about, Lucky was surprised to see
how big and sprawling the longpaw house was – nothing
like a cage. He felt almost free as he explored the rooms.
His claws clicked on the hard floor of the food area as
he nosed around the cupboards. There was a distinct,
though faint, smell of food – raw meat, soft cheese and
stale bread – but frustratingly, though he pawed at the
cold-box door, it refused to open for him. Scenting Bella
behind him, he turned to see her standing sheepishly in
the doorway, head lowered.

"I couldn't get into the cold-box either. And there were bits of food around the longpaw house, but I ate them. I should have left some, I know, but I was so hungry."

"Don't worry." It was true, she *should* have thought ahead; she should have avoided bolting everything down the first day – but Lucky reminded himself yet again that Bella didn't know any better. She was a Leashed Dog. Once again, he found himself grateful that he'd learnt to survive and look after himself. He wondered what would become of dogs like Bella in this new and hostile world.

"But it *was* stupid," she went on, ears drooping. "I should know better, Lucky. I *do* understand, even if some of the others don't."

"They've a lot to learn," he remarked.

"Please don't think too badly of them, Lucky." She gave him a beseeching gaze. "It's all they know – being carefree, never having to worry. I've never had to worry about my next meal either, but I do understand that's not how it is for every dog. I know things are different now." She turned and slunk out of the kitchen.

Unsettled, Lucky sat down and gave his ear a comforting scratch with a hindpaw. When he felt better he spent a few more moments sniffing and scratching at cupboard doors. He had another go at the cold-box. He raked at it with his paws and tugged with his teeth, until it felt as though they'd tear from his jaws, but it refused to open for him. He was wasting his time and energy. *I might as well make myself comfortable until tomorrow,* he thought, going in search of his litter-sister once more.

He didn't have far to look. Bella was just in the next room, which was furnished with tables and lamps and a longpaw picture box – though the hum of invisible power was absent. There was one of the soft longpaw seats that he'd made himself comfortable on before. But his litter-sister was crouched in a corner, sniffing mournfully at a small pile of longpaw things between her paws.

Lucky padded across to her. She barely stirred, only snuffled and whimpered at the scent on a burst cushion. There was a longpaw fur, too, crumpled and smelling of sweat, and a leather lead like the ones he'd seen attached to Leashed Dogs. The very sight of it made him shiver with distaste, but Bella was nuzzling it longingly.

She must have been entirely wrapped up in the memories the scent-things stirred, because when he licked her ears sympathetically, she jolted and scrambled to her four paws, avoiding his gaze.

"I'm just tired," she said gruffly. "These things. They help me sleep. That's all."

Lucky said nothing. How could a few longpaw

trinkets help a dog sleep? Perhaps the loss of the longpaws really was hard for her. If that was true, he had a notion she'd be too embarrassed ever to admit it.

"Come on," he said, touching her muzzle gently with his own. "We have to get some sleep. Who knows what a new sun-up will bring?"

It was obvious where she usually slept; beside the pile of treasure, nestled in this cosy corner, was a squashy cushion covered in shed golden hair and smelling strongly of Bella. Lucky waited for his litter-sister to tread a languid circle on it, then settle, head on her paws. Only then, with a polite whine, did he turn his own three careful circles, and close his eyes with a silent wish to the Sky-Dogs. He snuggled down beside his litter-sister and rested his head on her back.

It was warm in this corner, and the cushion moulded perfectly to their bodies, but Bella seemed unsettled, and her restlessness infected Lucky.

Lucky raised his head, opening his jaws a little to taste the air, and beside him Bella gave a soft whimper of unease. The atmosphere tasted familiar, somehow, and not in a good way. He recognised it, suddenly and horribly, as the way the air had tasted and felt before the earth had shuddered so violently. Before the Growl. There was that prickling sensation again, and the metallic smell of danger.

"I can't sleep here, Bella. I can't," Lucky whined, glancing around. "What if the longpaw house falls on us?"

"No. It won't happen. The Growl has gone." Bella flattened herself on the cushion, as if willing herself to go to sleep. "Don't be silly, Lucky. We'll be fine."

She was wide awake, though; Lucky could sense it. Again she fidgeted, and at last she got to her feet, head lowered, ears pricked for trouble.

"On the other paw ..." she murmured.

Lucky stood up, determined. He knew this warning in his bones; he knew this urge in his gut. "Higher ground, Bella. *Higher ground.*"

"Yes. You're right, Lucky. *Yes.*"

No sooner had she said it than the floor rippled beneath their paws. It felt like nothing more than the shiver of skin beneath fur, but the two dogs bolted for their lives. Crashing together as they leapt from the cushion, they stumbled, and Lucky took a moment to make sure Bella was back on her feet. They scrambled through the hallway, barged out of the open door and raced outdoors to safety. The Big Growl had left many of the doors hanging at awkward angles. Longpaws would have hated it, but it made it easy for the dogs to move around – thank goodness.

"We have to warn the others!" cried Bella.

But before they could so much as bark, the rest of the Leashed Dogs were running from their longpaws' houses too, darting into the open patch of grass in the middle of the houses. Unsure of themselves, afraid to make a further move in any clear direction, they circled, whined, scratched at the earth. Martha gave a deep bark at her own longpaw's house, and started back towards it. Daisy yelped frantically and began to race back to her home.

"No!" barked Lucky. "Stay together! Stay here!"

It wasn't much of a strategy, but it seemed like their safest option. Once again the other dogs looked at him in that trustful, appealing way that made his skin prickle. *No time to worry about it* … thought Lucky.

"Everyone together. Come on!" Lucky gave the most commanding bark he could muster, but no-one protested. The dogs crowded around him in a huddle, seeking safety and protection in the warmth and numbers of a …

… *Pack*, thought Lucky with a jolt.

The ground felt so terribly disturbed beneath his paw pads. It shook and quivered still, as if it was trying to throw them off. Was the Earth-Dog afraid of the Big

Growl too? Or were the two of them part of each other? Lucky didn't know. *Please*, he thought, *please, Earth-Dog, keep us safe ...*

Maybe the Earth-Dog listened to him, because the Big Growl didn't return – not the way it had that terrible night. This could have been its smaller earth-brother, turning restlessly the way Bella had, but going back to sleep in its underground den. The ground stopped grumbling beneath his paws, and the crackling sensation left the air. For the first time in ages, Lucky breathed properly. Around him the other dogs, too, were shaking the fear out of their fur, standing up more confidently, looking around for the next danger. They weren't assuming that all was well again, and they weren't trotting straight back to their longpaw houses, but they weren't panicking, and that made him absurdly proud of his whole ...

Don't think it, he told himself. *They're not my Pack.*

Yes he'd helped them, and maybe he'd found it reassuring to huddle together with other dogs. But that didn't mean a thing! They wouldn't have been much use to him if the danger had worsened.

Time to strike out again, Lucky told himself. *Alone.* His fate was in his own paws and he'd better remember it. Warm flanks were one thing, but there was a lot more to Pack life than a bit of company. A lot more, and some of it he couldn't bear to imagine …

And then he stopped worrying, because a new, deadly rumble filled the air. There wasn't time to huddle together and protect each other. The rumbling instantly became a tremendous crash, a chaos of stone and screeching metal, and the air filled with blinding dust.

Lucky froze, crouching against the ground, and so did the others. He gazed ahead, his jaw hanging slack. Where a longpaw house had stood, right next to Bella's, now there were only billowing clouds of smoke.

The echoing thunder seemed to go on forever. No one moved until the dust began to thin and clear and settle. Sunshine whimpered uncertainly, and Mickey's growl was a frightened one.

Nothing had fallen on them; he'd gathered Bella's friends in exactly the right place, he realised with pride. And just as well: he saw that straight away.

His sense of achievement was swept away as the hairs stood up on the back of his neck and shoulders. The sound that came from the ruins was horrible: an unearthly howl of terror and pain and desolation. For a few seconds he stood stock-still with the rest of them, uncomprehending, as chills ran through his belly; was the Earth-Dog herself mourning and whining at this further disaster? Was this the final straw: the destruction of all that was left?

Then, at his side, Bella lifted her muzzle and gave a hysterical howl. Lucky watched in amazement as she stood there, trembling, the others joining in her cry of distress.

"What?" he snapped desperately. "Bella! Tell me!"

"*Alfie!*" she whined. "He's trapped in that house!"

CHAPTER TEN

"Alfie! Alfieeeee!" Sunshine was running in frantic circles. "Lucky, do something! *Pleeeease!*"

Lucky turned from one dog to the other, nearly tripping over Daisy again. The other dogs were all frozen to the spot. "Who's Alfie?"

Bella shook her head miserably. "He's a brave little dog. He wasn't with us when we found you. He'd stayed behind to guard his longpaws' house!"

"I knew we should never have left him," Daisy muttered, her nose drooping into the dirt.

"There's nothing we can do." Mickey's whine was bleak.

"If we go in there we might be killed." Bella took a

shivering step backwards as she stared at the wreckage. A faint breeze lifted another billow of white dust, and another piece of wood creaked, fell and shattered. The howling rose again from the longpaw house: a small dog, lonely and desperate and afraid.

Martha raked the ground with one huge paw, unwilling to look at anyone. "Poor Alfie. He wasn't really one of us. He always kept himself to himself."

"Martha's right." Bella crouched on her belly, pawing dust from her eyes. "He wasn't one of our Pack, Lucky. Not really. Oh, poor little Alfie. If he'd only come with us … but he hardly ever did …"

Lucky looked from the collapsed longpaw house to the other dogs, and back again. Why were they talking about Alfie as if he was already dead?

He had to bark loudly to make himself heard over the miserable sound from the ruins. "What are you saying? There's a dog trapped in there! He's still alive!"

"But we can't help him." Bella's ears flattened even closer against her skull, and she growled resentfully. "We can't do anything!"

"We have to *try!*" snapped Lucky. Daisy was staring up at him with wide eyes.

Sunshine whined and spun frantically. "We can't leave him there, can we, Bella?" Her ears drooped.

"Can we?"

A deep gruff bark came from his side. Lucky turned, surprised, to see Bruno, stocky and belligerent.

"Lucky's right." Bruno glared at Bella and the others. "Alfie's one of our Pack whether he knows it or not. And I'm going to help!"

"Thank you," Lucky said. Bruno, at least, understood what it meant to look out for other dogs. "You'll make a good Pack member. Now, come with me."

As they both turned and loped towards the ruin, Sunshine's whimper rose behind them, high and frightened. "I'd come too. I'd come, but …"

Lucky shook his head. *They treat me like I'm some expert on being a Pack leader,* he thought, *and they don't even know what being in a Pack means!*

But if they wanted leadership, he'd give it to them; he'd show them this one last thing before moving on. Whatever else lay ahead of them, they'd have to find out for themselves, the hard way. *One last favour. No dog deserves to be left to die. Then I'm off – they can look after themselves!*

"Look at the front of the longpaw house," rumbled Bruno. "If he was in there, he'd be a dead dog already. He must be in the back, in the kitchen. The cold room, you know? That's where his basket was."

"Right. Good thinking, Bruno." Lucky inspected the ruins, pacing carefully through the debris. The walls were reduced to rubble at the front and sides of the longpaw house, and the roof had caved in completely. "There's still a wall standing around the back. Let's try there."

Lucky picked his way to the back, moving carefully on his injured paw pad. He could still hear Alfie howling pitifully somewhere under the rubble.

"Alfie! Can you hear me?" Bruno barked. Alfie's yelping didn't stop; his friend's calls to him had gone unheard.

They clambered over fallen bricks and pieces of twisted metal into the garden of the longpaw house.

Lucky sniffed at the ground. No invisible power here; its source must have been destroyed. A huge and creaking old tree overshadowed the yard, and he glanced up at it nervously. It leaned at a slight angle, its trunk cracked where the lower branches began to spread, and he didn't like the groaning noise that came from within it, as if it was in pain.

Just in time, he spotted the broken shards of clear-stone on the ground in front of his paws. He trod a delicate path around them, followed by Bruno. A window had fallen out of the back wall. In the empty space left, some criss-crossed wire was torn and sagging, but still intact.

"That's our way in." Lucky nodded at the window.

He put a paw against the wire mesh, but quickly drew it back. It felt so sharp, reminding Lucky of his Trap House cage. He couldn't afford a second wound – but Alfie's howls were a tormenting racket. The sound made Lucky's bones ache and his blood pound. *I can't give up!*

Lucky scrambled up on a pile of rubble, Bruno at his side. Together they tugged with their teeth, and Lucky tried scratching the stone aside with his claws, but it was no use. Lucky got a good grip on a sagging piece of mesh, but it sprang back, giving his nose a stinging blow. Lucky jumped away and tilted his head, frustrated.

"This is no good. What should we do now?" Bruno frowned.

Lucky realised that the proud old dog was deferring to his experience. He felt a flush of confidence surge through him. *I can do this.*

"I got it!" Lucky turned and bounded down from the pile of blocks. "I know what to do!"

"Lucky, look out!"

Lucky heard Bruno's shrill bark of alarm. He looked up in terror as the groaning tree gave a crack like the war of the Sky-Dogs.

He couldn't falter. He dashed on, dodging sideways

as the massive branch above him plummeted to the earth. It missed the tip of his tail by a hair's breadth; he felt the rush of air on his hindquarters.

As the crash of leaves and branches faded, he paused to glance back at Bruno, catching his breath. He gave a sharp bark of gratitude for the warning. Then he was running hard for Bella's house.

Bella and Sunshine barked something he didn't catch as he sprinted away from Alfie's home. The rest of the Pack was still huddled together on the grass patch in between the longpaw houses. Were they encouraging him, or trying to get him to stop? He didn't have time to think about it now. He reached Bella's door, and hesitated, his heart thrashing.

This longpaw house might collapse too. Lucky's forelegs trembled with nerves as he eyed the cracked walls.

I'd better be quick ...

Darting through the doorway, he found Bella's sleeping corner and snatched up her soft-hide in his jaws. It was big and thick, and awkward to carry, but it was perfect for what he had in mind. He dragged it out through the door, his muscles trembling with relief as he reached the open air once more. He paused, letting the pounding of his heart calm a little – and giving quick thanks to the Earth-Dog for her tolerance – then raced back to where Bruno waited, to where Alfie still whined pitifully for help.

"We're coming, Alfie," growled Bruno reassuringly. "Not long now! Stay calm."

Please, Earth-Dog, Lucky took a moment to beg, *will you help me again like you did in Bella's house? Please let us get Alfie out. Please don't let the Big Growl come for us …*

With the soft-hide between their teeth protecting their soft gums from the tearing spikes of wire, Lucky and Bruno tugged as hard as they could. Lucky felt his body jerk back as strands of wire weakened and tore apart. One last tug – and a whole section of wire was ripped aside.

Yes! We're in!

There were jagged spikes of broken clear-stone around the wooden frame, but the soft-hide cushioned those, too, and both dogs managed to squirm through and into the longpaw house.

Bruno stood on the rubble-strewn floor, panting from the exertion. "Alfie! Where are you?"

There was a soft whine from beneath one of the longpaws' sitting boxes. Lucky tugged at it with his jaws, loosening a tangle of broken wood and metal till they could reach the dog trapped beneath. Bruno squirmed between the wooden legs, grabbed Alfie's collar and dragged him free.

The little dog lay shivering for a few moments before getting shakily to his paws. He glanced nervously at Lucky. Alfie was like a smaller version of Bruno – just as stocky and blunt-faced – but his fur was jet black apart from two white forepaws.

"Thank you," he whispered, and glanced around sadly at his ruined house.

"Come on," grunted Bruno. "Let's get you back to the others."

Lucky led the way carefully back across the rubble-strewn floor and through the broken window. Bruno had to give Alfie a nudge up with his head just to help the little dog reach the windowsill.

"You'll have to stay with us now, Alfie," Bruno said, when they were safely outside.

"Yes … oh, my poor longpaws!" He whined with distress as he stared at the wreckage of his home. "Where are they, where *are they?* Look at this place! What will they do when they come back?"

Lucky blinked. Why were these Leashed Dogs so anxious about their longpaws' feelings? It wasn't as if the longpaws had given them much thought before they ran.

"Don't worry about them," he growled. "You have to take care of yourself for now."

Alfie's head was hunched into his neck as he looked up at Lucky, and he blinked anxiously. "Who are you?"

"He's Lucky," broke in Bruno. "And so are you. It's amazing you weren't crushed in there. Now come on."

The others were waiting, tense, ears pricked as they picked their way back to the grass in the middle of the avenue. Lucky gave each one of them a disdainful stare.

We saved him, no thanks to any of you ...

Bella came forwards and tentatively licked Lucky's ear. "I'm glad you're all right," she murmured guiltily.

He made a rumbling sound in his throat, not quite ready to forgive her. The others were avoiding his eyes, blinking around at the skewed walls of their longpaw houses, the dust clouds raised by a tiny breeze. The surroundings looked almost as forlorn as they did.

Sunshine was the first to recover. She trotted up to Alfie, licking him in apologetic welcome. Soon the others joined her, nuzzling the friend they'd nearly abandoned out of fear.

"You see, Bella?" whined Sunshine. "I knew Lucky would get him out! I knew he could do it!"

"I got him out too," grumbled Bruno.

"Of course you did! Brave Bruno!" Sunshine was

beside herself with admiration. "It was the right thing to do, Bella! You shouldn't have tried to stop them."

"Hey!" objected Martha. "You didn't want to help either, Sunshine!"

"Wait a minute." From the milling group of dogs, Alfie pushed forward, tilting his head to the side. "Bella?" he squeaked in disbelief. "Were you going to leave me there?"

The happy growls and yelps faded to a guilty silence. Bella hung her head.

"Alfie, you mustn't be angry with Bella," said Mickey. "She was right to be careful." He padded up beside her and nuzzled her neck. "We didn't know how dangerous the longpaw house was, and anything might have happened. Bruno and Lucky could have been killed, too. It was a tough decision, and she was thinking of everybody. Let's just be glad it worked out, and you're safe."

Bella licked the dog's black-and-white face gratefully and Alfie gave a reluctant nod. Lucky, though, kept silent, thinking.

What Mickey said was true. Bella's attitude had made sense. And yet ...

Hearing Alfie crying for help like that, Lucky couldn't have left him – the other dog's distress caused an urgency in his bones and blood, something he could not resist. There was an instinct, a dog-spirit deep inside him, and he was growing more aware how much he relied on its strength in times of danger.

So where did that leave Bella ...?

Lying down, head on his paws, Lucky watched his litter-sister sadly. The dog-spirit inside her was quiet, repressed, buried so deep she had forgotten it long ago. There were times when a dog had to rely on his inner spirit to tell him what to do – but Bella thought like a longpaw.

Anxious, he got to his feet and padded closer to her. She seemed uneasy, but then all of them did. Mickey pawed at his glove – Lucky finally recognised it now; it was like the ones he'd seen when longpaw pups played ball in the streets. Martha sat beneath the wilting tree, ears drooping. Sunshine nibbled at a few blades of grass, disconsolate, while Daisy padded back and forth, gazing at her creaking longpaw house and sniffing anxiously. Alfie simply lay with his head on his paws. He looked as though he was thinking hard.

They failed their first test as a Pack, thought Lucky. *And they know it.*

Lucky gave a soft growl and drew Bella aside.

She glanced at him, her tail wagging low to the

ground.

"Don't even say it, Lucky." She sounded bitter. "It's not that I didn't care. I didn't want any harm to come to Alfie. But I was afraid for the others. I was afraid for *you*."

"You don't have to make excuses to me, Bella." He'd meant it to sound kind, but she bristled.

"I'm not making excuses! I made a perfectly sensible decision, and you went against it. If you had been killed inside that longpaw house, it would have been your own fault."

"You don't need to worry about me! I can *always* look after myself – I'm used to it."

"But Bruno isn't. None of us are!" she snapped. "You have to understand, Lucky. We're not like you. I need to make my *own* decisions. You made the right one in the end with Alfie. But it might have been the wrong one! It could have been disastrous. So you don't need to tell me I was *wrong*."

Lucky stared at her, exasperated. "I know. The thing is, I think it's important that you –"

A wailing whine cut through the air, and all the dogs' heads snapped round to stare at Sunshine.

"Daisy!" she cried, turning one way, then the other, on the verge of yet another panic. "Where's Daisy? She's gone!"

CHAPTER ELEVEN

What trouble has Daisy got herself into? wondered Lucky.

Sunshine was dashing in frantic circles; Martha paced back and forth as Mickey tried to herd the group around Lucky. But the other dogs were too frantic to obey.

"We've got to look for her." Bruno said. "We've *got* to. But *where?*"

"We can't just stand by!" yelped Sunshine, and her ears drooped with shame as she muttered, "Not like last time."

"Bruno's right!"exclaimed Bella, "We need to think!"

Yes, thought Lucky, exasperated, *but none of you are!* He leapt up on to a tumble of bricks and gave a commanding bark.

"Calm down, all of you!" As they turned to gaze at him, Lucky shook his head. "Be quiet – all that noise doesn't help Daisy! I'll try to sniff her out. She can't be far away."

There was a line of longpaw houses to his left, low and neat behind trimmed lawns; they seemed to be less badly damaged than the others, though their windows were cracked and bits and pieces of walls had crumbled away. He took a few paces towards them, sniffing and cocking his ears, straining to find Daisy's trail. He was sure he'd seen her looking towards one of those longpaw houses while he and Bella fought: that one with the broken swing in the front garden and a lifeless stone rabbit on the doorstep, one ear snapped off.

Bella and Mickey were right behind him. *They don't want to be seen hesitating again.*

The others held back and watched, eyes beseeching. That didn't make it easier to concentrate – but there was something else, too, interfering with Daisy's scent. It was a sharp and strange odour that drifted in the air, sickening and dizzying.

A suggestion of Daisy pricked his nose, but he couldn't pin her down – not with that acrid smell making his head sway and his stomach churn. Lucky lifted his muzzle into the faint breeze, going absolutely still. That smell. It was coming from …

Daisy's house!

"Stay back!" he barked sharply. His hackles bristled; there seemed to be something treacherous about that sharp sickly scent. It wasn't the death-smell, but his instincts screamed at him to avoid it as if it was.

Padding cautiously towards Daisy's house, the smell grew overwhelming. His eyes watered, his stomach turned, and for an instant he was so light-headed he nearly stumbled.

But Daisy's scent was definitely there – almost buried beneath the dreadfulness …

And there she was! Swaying, but standing determinedly square, Daisy blinked at him from the skewed shadows of the cracked porch. Her eyes were unfocused, and she looked as if she might collapse at any moment.

Darting forward, Lucky snatched at her collar, his eyes streaming now, his sense of smell dead to everything but the sick-stench. She gave a little whimper as he lifted her by the scruff of her neck and turned, bounding back to the others. Even as he ran, Lucky felt his body wobble and sway, but the smell was already growing fainter as he bounded unsteadily back to the tight group of anxious dogs. When he could smell it no longer he let Daisy fall to the grass and stood over her, panting and staggering with dizziness.

She was asleep now, motionless on the ground, her flanks barely moving. Lucky began to lick her fiercely, and Bella moved to join him as the others looked on with fear.

"Why is she sleeping?" yelped Sunshine. "What were you running away from?"

"Come on, Daisy," Bella whined. "Wake up."

Her body lay as if lifeless, her sides moving almost imperceptibly with her breaths. They seemed to rise and fall less and less. How long would it take for her to stop breathing altogether? Her eyes had rolled back in her head and white flecks foamed at the corners of her mouth. Martha reached out with one of her giant, webbed paws. With more gentleness than Lucky could have imagined from such a huge dog, she wiped the foam from the corners of Daisy's mouth.

"Don't die!" Bella said, more urgently. She gently poked Daisy's body with her paw. Nothing.

"Come away," Lucky told his litter-sister. "It's best to leave her now." Whatever fighting spirit had been in Daisy had gone now. He started to turn away, his head bowed, when ...

"Wait!" Bella cried, drawing closer to Daisy. "Look!"

She was right. The little dog was trembling back into life. Her eyelids opened, and a shiver ran through her fur. A paw twitched, her tail thumped feebly, and her dark eyes opened. They were still blurry and distant, but Lucky felt a huge wave of relief as he sat back and watched Bella wash Daisy's face.

"Oh, Daisy. You're all right!" Bella nuzzled her. "What on earth happened? Where did you go?"

Unsteadily Daisy sat up, tilting her head from side to side as she tried to get her balance back. "I'm sorry. You were all fighting and I didn't want to listen."

Mickey paced forward to lick her nose. "What a time to go wandering!"

"I just thought, well, I'll go and see if my longpaw's house is all right, and … I smelled something odd …" Daisy shook herself, a little shamefaced, but her eyes were brightening once more, her ears were pricked and she looked steadier. "It was worse than anything I'd ever smelled before – even worse than the time I got sprayed by a skunk and had to sleep in the garage. I didn't know what it was, but I thought if I found out I could tell you all about it." Daisy looked sheepish. "It was coming from the kitchen. I went closer to get a better sniff at it, and … I felt so sick and dizzy. I thought you'd know what to do – but I couldn't seem to walk straight. I felt so awful."

The Sun-Dog was starting to come up over the broken roofs of the longpaw houses, and as Lucky looked around at the cracked and tottering walls and broken road, his fur bristled and he stood straighter.

"Listen, all of you." He looked around at them, meeting their eyes with determination. "You have to leave this place. Now. And for good."

"What are you talking about?" Bella barked, showing her teeth. "We can't leave!"

Lucky took a pace back. "Bella –"

"This is our *home!*" she snarled. "We have to wait for our longpaws. I don't expect you to understand, but we can't go. Not yet."

Lucky couldn't speak for a moment. No, he *didn't* understand. But her bark was so fierce it made his stomach clench.

The others' tails drooped, and they lowered their ears, looking from Bella to Lucky and back again. Bella looked ferocious, her hackles raised.

"But Bella …" whispered Daisy.

"No. Don't listen to him, Daisy! Lucky's a smart dog, but he's a Lone Dog. He doesn't understand about longpaws; he doesn't understand why we can't leave!" Bella bared her teeth at her brother. "I know you don't approve, Lucky, but we're loyal to our longpaws, and we can't abandon their homes."

"Bella!" he barked angrily. "In the name of the Sky-Dogs! Don't you understand? It's dangerous here – that smell nearly killed Daisy. Alfie's house collapsed. And it *isn't* Alfie's house," he added savagely. "It belongs to Alfie's longpaws, and Alfie's longpaws left him – like they left you all!"

Bella yelped in frustration, but she stood up to him defiantly. "They didn't mean to!"

Lucky stalked forward, curling his muzzle. "Oh, yes they did. These longpaw houses are falling down, Bella." He turned his head to give the buildings a look of distaste and fear. Against the dimming sky they seemed even more ominous, skewed and looming as if they'd crumble at any moment. "They won't be here for long, and that smell is a death-smell. It's like the breath of the Earth-Dog herself!"

Martha shivered with fear, and Sunshine gave a pitiful whine, but Bella scraped her claws along the earth for silence. "You are so superstitious, Lucky! The smell is – I don't know, but it's not the Earth-Dog."

Lucky shook his head, hackles bristling. "How do you know? How do we know what goes on down there in the darkness? If we're lucky, the Earth-Dog will protect us from the Big Growl. But what if she thinks we aren't worth protecting – that we're stupid mutts who aren't clever enough to sense danger? She might abandon us altogether!"

"You're talking nonsense!" Bella snapped.

Lucky growled. "This place could kill you. You can't stay here. Don't you all trust me, after everything we've been through? Haven't I gotten you out of trouble? Did your longpaws stay to do that?"

Someone whimpered in the silence that fell. The dogs' heads drooped and seven tails tucked between their legs. Even Bella looked downcast and, for the first time, uncertain.

"But where would we go?" Bruno asked.

"I don't know." Lucky sat down, scratching his ear to dispel the aggravation he felt. "I suppose you could come with me, just for a bit. Or you could lead your friends somewhere else, Bella. I know you could do it."

"I don't," she murmured.

"But whatever happens," he went on, "you have to find a new place to live. You understand, don't you?"

Daisy's tail thumped slowly and pitifully on the grass, raising puffs of dust. "But if we go – if we leave here – how will they find us? How will our longpaws find us when they come back?"

Lucky gave a bitter snarl. "You need to *give up* on your longpaws!"

He turned to glare at her – and saw that her eyes were dark and huge. Beside her, Sunshine looked just the same – miserable, needy and desperate for reassurance. Lucky breathed out, forcing himself to calm down. He was asking a lot of them, after all. Their comfortable lives had spoiled them. They weren't just Leashed Dogs – they were Spiritless Dogs.

Lost Dogs.

Quietly he growled, "If the Earth-Dog is still angry, if the Big Growl might return, we need to leave. You know it's true – feel it inside you. Stop thinking like longpaws – feel the dog-spirit. It's there somewhere, I promise." Affectionately he licked Daisy's face, and put more confidence into his voice than he really felt. "You'll be fine. You're strong dogs, I know it. One day, your longpaws might come back. When you see other longpaws returning, and this place feels safe again, you can come back too."

Inside his belly he felt a twist of guilt at his lie. He was certain that their longpaws would never return – why would they? Their homes were ruined and belongings destroyed. But for now, he knew these dogs needed to believe the longpaws were coming back for them.

Pricking his ears with confidence, he gazed at them.

One by one they whined, lowered their heads in acknowledgement, and thumped their tails sadly.

"Yes," said Bella at last. "You're right. This place is dangerous. We'll come with you. But there's something we need to do first. Things we need to get."

She nodded to the other dogs, who all turned and padded towards their longpaw houses. Only Mickey stayed where he was at Lucky's side, silent and patient.

Lucky watched them go. Hadn't he convinced them yet? What in the name of the Sky-Dogs could they be doing now?

"Daisy!" he barked, as he realised that the little dog was heading for her own foul-smelling yard. "What are you doing? You can't go back in there!"

"I just need to get something," Daisy yapped back. Lucky watched in astonishment as she took a deep breath and then ran across the grass into the longpaw house. He couldn't help but hold his breath until she re-emerged, clutching something in her mouth.

One by one, each dog came out of their longpaw house carrying something. Not one of the objects looked as if it would be of any practical use. Martha's powerful jaws now gripped a red square of cloth. Sunshine had retrieved a yellow leather leash studded with sparkling stones, and Daisy a battered leather pouch, one of those longpaw treasure pouches he'd seen before. Unable to go back into his collapsed longpaw house, Alfie had lifted a rubber ball sorrowfully from his littered front yard; Bruno's square jaws dripped drool, wetting the peaked longpaw cap he held.

Now he could see why Mickey hadn't gone with the others: he had simply kept hold of his padded glove.

As for Bella, she gazed defiantly at Lucky as she set down a tatty stuffed bear-toy at his forepaws. "These things still smell of our longpaws," she told him in a low growl. "We need something to remind us."

Hesitantly, Lucky eyed each object, then nodded. They were at least trying to do what was right; perhaps he needed to make allowances for them and their sad Leashed pasts.

"Of course," he said, licking her nose to show that he understood. "Of course you can bring them along. Now follow me. Mickey – you bring up the rear, you're good at that. We'll head into the hills."

As they padded silently through the outlying streets, Lucky tried not to look back at the city where he'd run happily free. Bad enough that the other dogs halted, now and again, to gaze back mournfully at their old lives. That bustling, lively place of the longpaws was wrecked and gone, and they were leaving it forever. Distantly a loudcage howled; in a far street iron groaned and clear-stone shattered as another wall fell. Otherwise there was only silence, and the death-smell.

There was no looking back. No looking back at all ...

CHAPTER TWELVE

As their surroundings grew less city-like, and the longpaw houses were scattered further and further apart, Lucky's spirits lifted. He'd forgotten how much he enjoyed the freedom and space of the wild – on the rare occasions when he ventured there.

He'd gone past the city limits only a few times: for the chase of a rabbit-hunt; or when the longpaws from the Trap House were on the streets and he needed to make himself scarce for a few days. Now, he felt excitement growing in his belly and tickling his spine. He could try proper hunting again – rabbits, squirrels, even gophers!

This wasn't wild country just yet, but it was getting that way. A scrubby field lay before them, rough-grassed and fenced with broken wire. Not the wilderness, but not a longpaw park, either. Running through the gorse and weeds was a small sluggish river, perhaps two dog-lengths wide, its surface calm and smooth and slow. Lucky's ears pricked up and he panted with pleasure as the other dogs came to his side.

"Water!" he said, and bounded towards it.

He was still many dog-lengths away from it when he scrabbled to a halt, hair bristling all over his body, the river-smell stinging his nostrils. A growl rumbled in his throat.

Bella slowed too, and stopped beside him, one paw still raised. She sniffed the air, suspicious, as the others joined them.

"There's something wrong," she whined.

"Something *very* wrong," Lucky confirmed, backing slowly away from the glistening stream.

"What could possibly be wrong?" With a howl of joy, Alfie darted past them all, nearly knocking Sunshine over in his haste. "Come on!"

"Alfie, no!" Lucky sprang after the squat little dog. Alfie was dashing at his top speed, but Lucky was faster.

Good thing Alfie has short legs, he thought grimly as he bounded almost on top of the smaller dog and seized him by the scruff of the neck.

Alfie struggled and wriggled in shock, paws flailing at the river. "Let me go! Let me go!"

Grimly Lucky turned and trotted back to the frightened group of dogs. They had come a little closer to the water, alarmed for Alfie's sake, but they were all sniffing the air now, shivering, their hackles high. He dumped Alfie unceremoniously at their paws, and the little dog scrabbled to his feet, shaking himself rid of the indignity.

"Don't you smell it, Alfie?" Martha shook her head at him. "That water isn't good."

"When is water ever bad?" he said indignantly. "My longpaws' water was always perfectly good!"

"Your longpaws' water was made safe and delivered in pipes," growled Lucky. "Come here. But *don't* touch the river."

He nudged Alfie to the river's edge, followed by the rest, who held back nervously from the odd sharp scent of the water. "You see? Look at it!"

Beside him he felt Alfie shiver. "That can't be right."

The river looked even more sluggish and stagnant up close, and its water wasn't clear, but a dense, impenetrable grey-green. Worst of all, it had grown a skin with pools of odd colours, like the stripes that lit the sky after a heavy rainfall. Lucky had seen this kind of water before – when a loudcage had been wounded, and bled on to the road and into puddles – but this was much worse. And though he disliked the scent of loudcage blood, it was nothing like as bad as this – a thick sickly stench that burned his nostrils.

"That's not a river at all," said Martha, shuddering.

Lucky glanced at the big Newfoundland in surprise, then back at the river. *She's right,* he realised.

"I think it's one of the scratches the Big Growl put in the earth. I nearly fell into one." Lucky trembled at the memory. "But this one's filled up with water from somewhere. It only *looks* like a river."

Bella growled with fear. "Let's get away from here. And don't be so impulsive again, Alfie! You've got to *listen.*"

Alfie looked suitably cowed by his scolding. "All right, Bella. I'm sorry."

They all turned and trotted back across the field, but they were only halfway to the tumbledown fence when Bruno pricked his ears and stopped, startled.

"Longpaws!" he exclaimed.

All the dogs stopped at once, cocking their ears to hear what Bruno had heard. Lucky could pick up longpaw voices, coming from somewhere across the scrubby field. There were quite a few of them, but what kind of longpaws would be gathering in a pack near that poisonous river?

His heart raced and he longed to run in the other direction, but the others didn't look worried at all. They were sniffing eagerly in the direction of the voices.

Sunshine yelped with delight. "Let's go say hello!"

"Where are they? Where are they?" Daisy screeched, spinning with overexcitement.

"Calm down," barked Lucky anxiously. "Don't draw attention! Be careful, all of you. *Calm down!*"

They ignored him. Martha, Mickey and Bruno were all giving deep, joyous barks, and Bella was looking towards a corner of the field, panting, her ears pricked forward with enthusiasm.

"There! There they are! By that big tower!"

Lucky froze. Yes, longpaws – yellow-suited, black-faced longpaws! He remembered them from the encounter in the city. They were *not* friendly, and their strange hides and eyeless faces made him prickle with nerves. "Wait –"

Too late.

"Oh, hurray!" Daisy gave a volley of barks, then raced towards the longpaws.

"Daisy!" yelped Martha in alarm.

All the dogs chased after her, Bella in the lead, but

Daisy had a huge head start, and her excitement gave her short legs an astonishing speed. The others weren't halfway to the longpaws when she reached them and bounced and leapt, yapping, around their booted feet.

The longpaws ignored her, Lucky noticed with relief as he ran. Maybe she would take the hint and leave them alone ...

Daisy was not to be ignored, however. When her friendly yelps got no reaction, she took hold of the shiny yellow hide on one longpaw leg, and tugged and shook it playfully.

The longpaw jumped back, shocked – and before Lucky could bark a warning, he had roughly shaken the little dog off. Daisy howled and tumbled on to the ground.

"Daisy!" Sunshine yelped.

Stupid longpaws! Lucky suppressed a growl and put on a burst of speed. He could see Daisy quivering as she tried to get back to her paws.

The yellow-hide longpaws were already turning to leave, talking urgently among themselves and comparing their beeping sticks. Lucky dashed up to Daisy, who was scrambling shakily to her feet.

"I have to ... but ... the longpaws ..." she took a step forwards, her eyes on the retreating longpaws. Lucky's heart sank as he realised she was still trying to follow them.

"No, Daisy!" He planted himself in front of her, blocking her way.

The little dog looked bewildered and shocked rather than hurt. "Why did the longpaw do that? I have to –"

"No, don't follow!" Bella was beside her now, too, licking her side where the longpaw had kicked her. "Leave them!"

The other dogs drew close, forming a cluster around Daisy, all of them sharing dazed and shocked glances.

"That's not how longpaws behave!" cried Martha.

"I don't understand," whined Sunshine mournfully.

"I've never seen a longpaw try to hurt a dog," said Mickey, shocked.

Lucky shook his head, astounded at their naivety. "I have," he growled darkly.

Bella gave him a worried glance, but she was more concerned with Daisy, who was sitting up now and whimpering. "Don't worry, Daisy. Those weren't our longpaws, or anything like them. Did you see their strange fur? Their faces?"

"Let's get away from here." Martha gently nudged Daisy away.

Lucky began to follow the others as they padded

dejectedly back the way they'd come, but he noticed Mickey wasn't following. "Mickey, come with us!"

Mickey turned to him. "There's something behind those longpaws being here all alone. I can feel it." He walked up to Lucky and growled in a low voice, "What were they doing?"

"I don't know," admitted Lucky. "I've seen hundreds of longpaws in the city, but I've never seen those beeping sticks before. And it looked like they wanted to find out about the strange river – why else would they stand so close to the bad water?"

"I don't like it." The black-and-white dog shook his head. "Those are the only longpaws we've seen since the Big Growl! Where are all the others?"

"They ran away…"

"But they didn't come back. Those longpaws did, but no one else. It's very odd, Lucky, and I don't like it."

I don't like it either, Lucky admitted to himself. *But who can explain longpaws? They aren't like us, whatever these dogs may think …*

"I don't have any answers," he said at last, "but I do know one thing: we need to get as far from here as we can. Come on, Mickey. The sooner we get well away from the city and into the wild, the safer we'll be."

CHAPTER THIRTEEN

This is my home now, Lucky thought as he padded determinedly further from the city. *The wild.*

They'd been walking for a long time since leaving the field of the longpaws and the poisoned river.

Only when he'd reached the crest of the first foothill did he turn, panting as he gazed back at what was left of the city. He'd rarely seen his former home from this distance before. It looked so strange now – its remaining buildings leaning forward dangerously, water spraying from angry cracks, and huge, glinting shards of metal piercing the sky. Craters had opened and taken great gulps of his city. Were there other Leashed Dogs back there, trying to survive amongst the ruins? They didn't stand a chance without their longpaws. *Everything has changed forever.*

It was just as well he'd allowed himself that one pause to look back, though. His odd gang of followers was having trouble keeping up, straggling in a long line behind him. Sunshine caught his eye, far back at the rear. For perhaps the sixth time she'd got her long white fur – not quite so white now – tangled in a thorn bush. Exasperated, he bounded back to her and pulled at the branches with his teeth to free her. As a strand of her fur tugged loose, she yelped.

"That hurts!"

"Calm down. It's not the end of the world!"

"Oh, so you're *happy* my fur's falling out? Just *look* at me!"

Ignoring her, he trotted back to his lead position. It wasn't just Sunshine. *These dogs,* he thought, *whined a lot.*

"You're doing fine!" he barked at them. It was a lie worthy of the cunning Forest-Dog himself. "Keep going. Don't give up."

Lucky looked at the rest of the dogs thoughtfully. He was worried that they were completely at a loss out here in the wild. Had a single one of them ever had to catch their own food, find their own safe shelter? *They wouldn't last for more than a few hours without me*, he thought. *First sign of a rainstorm and they'd scamper back to their ruined homes.*

Even as he hesitated and glanced back over his shoulder, he saw Alfie stumble to a halt yet again and flop to the ground.

"Is it time for a rest?" the little dog yelped.

"Look at my fur!" wailed Sunshine, scratching hopelessly at her belly.

"Sunshine, shut up!" snapped Bella. "This is no time to be whining!"

"Now, now," said Mickey, plodding tiredly up to the others and dropping his glove so that he could nudge them together with his nose. "We're all together. One, two, three ... yes, yes ... and Daisy. Good! Lucky, could we stop a little more often? It's hard keeping everyone together ... and my paw pads ache ..."

Lucky sat back on his haunches and glared at them. He'd been delighted that Mickey was helping – guarding the rear, rounding up the stragglers. And now even he was complaining!

"We have to keep moving!" Lucky barked.

"But *why?*" whimpered Alfie.

Standing up, Lucky shook himself, trying to get rid of his frustration. His instincts were screaming at him to keep going. "We can't stop for any old reason – just because some dog's paw aches, or you're a little out of breath! This isn't a stroll on a leash – this is getting as far away from danger as we can. Do you want to live or die? Stop for a rest and you'll soon meet Earth-Dog, I promise you that."

Some of the dogs let out low whimpers.

"Lucky's right," said Bruno encouragingly. "Come on."

They were still whining softly as they set off once more, gripping their longpaw things in their mouths, but Lucky tried his best to push their moans to the back of his mind. It was becoming harder and harder to feel sorry for them, even for Bella, who was on edge with everyone. She was curt and short-tempered with Lucky, snapped out orders at Mickey and Martha, and scolded the smaller dogs relentlessly.

"Sunshine! If you can't stop getting tangled, stay away from the thorns, you silly dog!"

Lucky might have tried to defend Sunshine – if he hadn't been so cross with her himself. He did his best to ignore both her and Bella. At least his own paw wound was feeling better, and he could set a good pace and example. If he'd been struggling too, they never would have got out of the city at all.

Bella had the energy of a bad mood to keep her going, and for a while Lucky was content to let her take the lead. She trotted ahead, her leg muscles working fiercely. He could almost hear the angry thoughts tumbling around inside her head. He fell back to keep an eye on the others, trotting beside Mickey.

"Thanks for herding everyone together back here," he said. "We can't afford to lose anyone."

"No worries. It's what I do," Mickey mumbled through the glove in his mouth. He shifted it slightly so that he could talk more easily. "It's good of you to lead us like this."

"Only for a little while," said Lucky quickly. Anxiety prickled through him – he couldn't let Mickey start thinking of him as Pack leader. He needed them to be strong without him. "You know, you'd all do much better without these longpaw things."

Mickey nodded, but he kept his grip on the glove. "I know. But I can't leave this. My young longpaw … he …"

When Mickey looked round at him, there was such sadness in his brown eyes that Lucky could almost feel it too. He shook his head. "I'm glad my longpaws gave me up," he said softly to the older dog, "I'm glad I didn't have a life like yours. All your longpaws have done is break your hearts." Lucky knew he was being harsh, but

Mickey deserved to hear the truth.

"But they never meant to, Lucky. If my longpaws left me, it was because they had no choice. I know that."

Lucky sighed. "All the same. I'm glad I never got the chance to be attached to mine."

Mickey gave him a sympathetic look. "Bella told me about what happened to you. They don't sound like any longpaws I've known."

"Hmph," growled Lucky.

"It's true. Most longpaws are good. My longpaws took care of me when I was sick. They fed me treats from the table, they took me to the dog park every day and played with me. The youngest pup – I slept in his bed every night, since I was a pup myself. I was on duty, you see, to stop him from having nightmares. But I had nightmares too. And then they stopped, because we both helped each other. That's what most longpaws are like. They're our friends."

"Lucky you," growled Lucky. It did sound nice, he thought, if you liked that sort of thing – but why did they abandon Mickey?

The city was fading into a haze behind them, the crumpled buildings and broken metal no longer visible. Lucky couldn't help feeling satisfied that despite all the whining, they'd managed to walk so far. If there were any more earth growls, they'd be far from those dangerous snakes that buzzed with energy or the falling blocks of stone that could crush a dog's body. The Sun-Dog was beating hard, and all around was the sound of crickets, but further ahead he could see pools of shade and scrubby patches of woodland. He lifted his muzzle, sniffing the faint breeze.

Could it be?

Yes! He knew that fresh scent, the teasing deliciousness of it. Water! And not bitter, rotten, grey-green water. Suddenly his throat felt dry, and the vision of a bubbling spring was too much to resist. He bounded ahead, barking.

"Come on! Come on! There's a river ahead!"

As if the Sky-Dogs had suddenly given them wings, the Pack burst forward, breaking one by one into an excited run. Lucky, racing side by side with Bella, crested a low rise – and there, glittering in the sun-high light, a clear stream flowed over stones.

"Is it safe?" barked Alfie anxiously. "Do you think it's poisoned?"

"Not this one," cried Lucky. "Use your nose! It smells fresh."

"He's right. I can smell the fish wriggling," said Sunshine. Lucky blinked at her in surprise. He could smell it too, but he wouldn't have expected the inside dog to recognise the scent. Sunshine must have a better sense of smell than he'd realised …

"Come on," he barked, and joyfully sprang for the deepest pool he could spot, plunging in up to his neck. He called to the others. "Look! This will make you feel better!"

Bella splashed in beside him, her temper forgotten. She and the other bigger dogs entered the water up to their bellies, lapping happily, shaking their fur free of dust and easing the ache of their paw pads. Alfie trotted deeper, sending up fountains of spray to splash the others, but no one minded. Little Daisy and Sunshine were more hesitant, but they paddled into the shallows, flicking droplets at one another's faces, panting and lapping and standing dreamily with water dripping from their jaws before wading further. Sunshine even let herself sink up to her shoulders, so the running water could wash her fur clean of the dirt. "Oh, this is lovely! Much better than that poisoned river!"

"Careful," warned Lucky. "River-Dog can be tricky, even when she's bringing you wonderful clean water. The stream's deeper when you go further in, and the flow looks fast."

They were far enough away from the city to stop and

rest for a little while, he decided. Wading from the water to join Bella on the pebbly shore, Lucky shook himself dry in a spray of cold droplets, and let the dappled light warm his fur.

Sunshine had splashed back out of the river, and was examining her paw doubtfully. Lucky sniffed at it with her.

"It's nearly healed," she said, sounding surprised.

"Clean it again," Lucky told her. "Just to be sure. Give it a lick. That's what I kept doing."

Gratefully she licked at the little scratch, as Alfie shook water from his short black fur and watched with interest.

"I can't believe Sunshine has a battle scar!" exclaimed Alfie." "I missed so much excitement!"

"You had quite a bit yourself," Bella reminded him.

"That's probably why I'm so hungry!" Sitting back on his sturdy haunches, he wagged his tail and looked expectantly at Lucky.

Alarmed, Lucky averted his eyes from Alfie's – which were big and hopeful – and studied the others instead, jumping and clambering out of the river. But they, too, were watching him with hope, tongues hanging out.

Oh no … thought Lucky. "I don't have food! Don't look at *me* like that!"

"Of course not!" panted Mickey, cocking his head to smile at Lucky. "But you can hunt!"

"Yes!" squealed Daisy. "You're a hunter! You can teach us!"

A chorus of barking approval greeted this statement, and Lucky felt his stomach shrink inside him. "I'm – I'm not a teacher! I don't know how ..."

"All you have to do is show us!" barked Mickey excitedly. "We'll copy you!"

"Yes!" squeaked Sunshine. "Go on, catch something!"

Dumbfounded, Lucky licked his chops. He was hungry, too, and though he wasn't a skilled hunter, he probably knew more than they did. He had all Old Hunter's teaching to fall back on. At the very least, he could make something up; it wasn't as if the Leashed Dogs would spot his mistakes ...

He took a deep breath. "Well, it's not that easy, Sunshine, but let's see ..." Lucky glanced around, deciding to start with the likeliest hunters. That would be Mickey, and Bella, and ... "Where's Bruno?"

They heard the splash. It wasn't the light happy splash of a dog playing in water. It was a great disastrous explosion of water.

"Bruno!"

They all raced to the water's edge. Daisy was yapping like crazy.

"I told him it was deep there! I told him he was too big and heavy!"

Lucky took a few steps into the rushing current, feeling it dragging at his paws. Out in midstream and already washed quite a way down, Bruno surfaced, his boxy head struggling to stay above the water, his paws and body thrashing wildly against the strength of the flow. His eyes rolled over towards them, silently pleading; then he sank and lurched up once again, gasping for air.

"Bruno!" barked Lucky. As he waded towards the deeper water, the current almost pulled his paws from under him. He froze, bracing himself on the slippery pebbles, and watched Bruno's struggles in desperation. They might both drown, and then what would happen to the Pack?

Oh, River-Dog, please help me! Don't take Bruno like this!

Just as he was about to fling himself into the deep centre of the stream, he saw a huge black shadow pound past him, scattering pebbles and plunging into the water, sending up a great fan of glittering droplets as her body submerged.

Martha!

They were all barking now, urging her back to shore, but Martha had surfaced mid-current and was swimming towards Bruno. The speed of the water was carrying her quickly, but she showed no sign of panic, her body cutting strongly through the foaming waves till she was alongside him. Lucky watched in awe.

Bruno didn't seem to notice her, too focused on keeping his ungainly head above the surface and snatching gasps of air as the water tumbled him helplessly. But Martha snatched the scruff of his wrinkled neck and dragged him through the water.

His eyes opened wide in surprise, but Lucky could tell that he was exhausted and panic-stricken. He gave only a brief startled wriggle, then went limp in her broad jaws. Even against the current, Martha swam powerfully to the bank downstream and tugged Bruno after her on to dry land.

The others raced down the stony riverbank, leaping logs and bushes to reach the two sodden dogs. Bruno lay panting and sneezing and coughing, head on the stones, his forepaws sprawled in front of him. Martha, though, barely showed a sign of strain. She was standing up, all concern for Bruno, shaking the water off her coat and licking the bulldog dry.

She's a real fighter, Lucky thought, impressed.

"Martha?" Bella had skidded to a halt. "Are you all right?"

"Of course I am," rumbled Martha. "Do you think Bruno's OK? Is he hurt?"

"He'll be fine." Lucky snuffled and licked at Bruno's muzzle, then stared again at the huge black dog with awe. "You swim. You swim *so well.*"

"Yes, that was amazing!" Daisy said. The other dogs were staring at Martha, slack-jawed.

Martha wagged her tail, and let her tongue loll as she looked at her paws. Lucky looked at them too, and felt his eyes widen. Between her claws, spread on the uneven pebbles of the beach, he could see …

Is that, is that …? It's webbed skin! He'd only ever seen skin like that on the water birds that lived on the ponds in the longpaw parks. He glanced back up at her face, but she didn't seem to see anything wrong as she stared awkwardly at her own paws, embarrassed by the praise.

Bruno was struggling to stand now, licking Martha's legs and lowering his muzzle in gratitude.

Well, River-Dog, Lucky thought, sending his thoughts out towards the bubbling water. *You may not have come to my aid yourself, but you must know Martha well …*

It was the best sign he could have had. Martha

had knowledge of the River-Dog that he couldn't have guessed at, and she clearly had her respect, too. She could survive out there. Maybe the others, too, had their own hidden links with the Dogs of Nature; connections just waiting to be reawakened.

For the first time since leaving the city, Lucky felt happy. He wouldn't be bound to these dogs forever, because there would come a time when they wouldn't need him. This funny, temporary Pack of his was going to make it – however much the world had changed. There'd come a day when they didn't need him any more, and then he'd be free again. Truly free.

CHAPTER FOURTEEN

The whimpering. Why didn't it stop? Why did it have to go on, and on …? Lucky couldn't bear it.

Yes, he was a coward! Yes, he should beg the Sky-Dogs to forgive him. But what could he do? Surely they couldn't expect him to sacrifice himself? The River-Dog couldn't expect him to die, when – when Bruno –

No! This wasn't right …

This wasn't Bruno! Those whimpering dogs weren't drowning. They weren't in the water at all! They were trapped in the rubble, caught and crushed when the Trap House fell. There was nothing he could do. He and Sweet were helpless. If they went back for the others, they would die too …

– Come on, Lucky!

Sweet! He ran blindly after her, his legs working hard, his heart pumping. He was desperate to block out the whimpering, the dying howls …

But there was something else. Another set of paws. Something behind him, pursuing him, running him down. It was angry, vengeful, merciless, and it was almost upon him.

This couldn't be right!

Lucky risked a glance behind him, even as he fled, lungs aching for air, muscles screaming for rest.

There was nothing behind him. Nothing but darkness in the city streets, shadows and broken light and destruction.

Then, out of the corner of his eye … glinting eyes and teeth. So many savage dogs, hunting him down. Howling, baying, they were almost on him, almost at his tail, jaws snapping, reaching out their jaws to seize him and tear him –

The Storm of Dogs –

Terror sent Lucky leaping to his feet so suddenly that he stumbled and almost fell. His chest and lungs heaved, and he panted, his throat parched. In his head he could still hear that ferocious baying, the sound of hate. It felt so real – but nothing like this had ever happened to him!

It wasn't a memory. *But what was it?* It didn't feel like a normal dream – it was too real.

As the fear drained from his body, his trembling died down and he watched the Leashed Dogs sleep. They'd settled down in a low hollow by the river – a sheltered spot, well hidden by the dip of the ground, but with no nearby rocks or gullies for enemies to lurk unseen. The dogs were far enough from the water to be safe, but close enough for the whispering rush of its voice to soothe them. Now the dawn was turning the river's surface pearly, and as Lucky watched, a fish jumped, then splashed beneath the rippling waves. Pale light glowed between the tree trunks, picking out the horizon in grey and pink and orange.

Gradually Lucky's breath calmed, and he licked his chops self-consciously. He felt ashamed of leaping to his feet, of being scared by the pictures in his mind. The other dogs all slept so peacefully, none of them haunted by ghost-hounds and demon-dogs. *It's just me. I'm the only one stupid enough to be fooled by my dreams.* Shame flooded him. Perhaps missing a meal last night had been foolish, but they'd all been too exhausted to hunt or eat. They'd all collapsed in a heap, but maybe Lucky's empty stomach had given him bad dreams.

Perhaps those memory-objects were helping the other dogs after all – those longpaw belongings. Perhaps they protected their dreams. Or perhaps it wasn't so surprising they didn't have nightmares since they were so far detached from their own dog-spirits.

It was true that Lucky himself wasn't exactly an expert on the natural world after his life spent scavenging for food in the city, but he was far closer to his dog-spirit than they were. And he felt it wakening more and more out here in the wild, thrilling in his belly and bones, keeping him alert and safe.

Lucky shivered. All his optimism, all his positive thoughts about Martha and the River-Dog had dissolved with the dream. *How could I possibly expect them to cope alone?*

It was a bleak thought, but he felt a new determination. He couldn't save the Trap House dogs when the Big Growl had first hit. But he *could* help these dogs. He could teach them to look after themselves. Perhaps that was what the Spirit Dogs were trying to tell him when they sent these dreams … If he helped Bella and her friends, maybe the bad dreams would stop.

It's worth a try, he thought. *Anything to stop the visions.* But even as he considered this, he knew it was too simple. There was more to those dreams.

There was a message.

He had to look after the Pack. No one else would. He had to look after them because something bad was coming; Lucky knew it in his marrow. He gave an involuntary shudder that wiped away any doubt about the startling dreams. They weren't just dreams; he'd been right to trust in them. They were warnings of something terrible, and not just for him: for all dogs. The *Storm of Dogs* ...

Lucky could hear his Mother-Dog's voice, from long ago: *"When the world turns upside down and the rivers run with poison ..."*

He shivered again, looking over at the Leashed Pack. They were barely able to survive in the wild ... if the *Storm of Dogs* was really coming, they'd never survive. He needed to help them learn to survive, and quickly!

Lucky let the others sleep on; why shouldn't they enjoy a few moments of peace? But soon the Sun-Dog had risen, glowing through the branches of the scrubby trees, and he couldn't wait any longer. Nudging at the dogs with his nose, whining gently, he goaded them all to their feet.

"Wake up! If you want to learn how to be good hunters, you need to get used to early starts."

Sunshine protested, covering her eyes with her

paws as she tried to snuggle back under Martha's belly, but the big black dog stood up and licked the little white one till she was awake and grumbling. Daisy woke with a start and almost immediately began to spin, panting with excitement. Bruno stretched his limbs tentatively, as if testing for injuries, but his soaking seemed to have done him no harm. Mickey and Alfie shook off sleep as Bella affectionately nudged Lucky's muzzle.

"I'm hungry," complained Sunshine, blinking dismally.

"If anyone wants breakfast," Lucky pointed out dryly, "we're going to have to catch it."

To his surprise, they accepted that without a murmur, and set off purposefully, after leaving their longpaw things carefully hidden beneath rocks or behind clumps of grass. The trees became sparser as the dogs trotted up the shallow slope away from the river, and as they crested a ridge, the woods gave way to a broad rolling grassland dotted with scrub and small rocks, and pocked with promising burrows.

The sight was encouraging – as was the swift movement of creatures disappearing below ground – and Lucky felt a flicker of pleasure pass over him. Today had a purpose. The tricky business of teaching these dogs, soft from longpaws spoiling them, how to hunt. The task would be sure to chase away the last clinging horrors of his dream.

"Now," he told them in a low voice as they sniffed hopefully at the breeze. "Try to be quiet and still – no sharp movements. That means you, too, Sunshine! Stay out of the eyeline of those burrows if you can – we need the gophers to think they're safe so they'll come back out of their holes."

"That makes sense to me!" said Mickey eagerly.

"Keep your noses alert for anything we can eat – gophers, rabbits, mice, anything – and try to hold on to the scent as you follow it to the source. Really open your nostrils – like this, see?" He flared his own, taking deep breaths, casting around in the wind. "It's easy once you start. Let's go."

It wasn't as if he was the most natural of hunters, but Lucky felt like the favoured pup of the Forest-Dog as he led the others in search of prey. Sunshine, despite his special warning to her, was incapable of doing anything quietly, yelping every time she so much as caught her fur on a twig. Alfie darted ahead, his little white paws flashing as he ran.

Mickey, Bella and Bruno were doing their best – slinking low to the ground, avoiding twigs and rustling brush as they snuffed the air for clues – but they weren't used to staying unseen. Though he didn't like to say so, Lucky knew they didn't have a hope of creeping up on the small prey they needed to catch. As for Martha, she was simply too big and burly to be inconspicuous – though Lucky couldn't resent her for that, not after what she'd done the previous day. They were such a varied bunch, he would simply have to accept that they all had different talents.

In the meantime, though, he had to give up any hope of rabbit or squirrel, any of which must have scarpered long ago, or of the gophers coming out of their holes. The land spread before them, not a mouse stirring, the only sound the breath of the wind in the grass.

We're wasting our time, he sighed inwardly. Calling them together again, he decided on a change of tactic.

"Let's start small," he suggested. "We'll practise with bugs and beetles."

"Bugs and *beetles?*" Sunshine's wail of horror must have frightened away any remaining prey. Lucky took a deep breath and reminded himself to stay patient.

"Yes. You don't have to eat them if you aren't that hungry," he said.

That quietened the little dog down.

"Here." Lucky pawed a rock, hooking it with his claws till it tumbled over to reveal fresh wet earth. "Catch,

Martha!"

She bounded forward, slapping both huge forepaws down on the beetles that scurried in a panic for the grass. Tentatively she lifted a webbed paw, and yelped with delight when two bugs tried to escape. Quickly she caught them again.

"Two!" exclaimed Lucky. "Well done, Martha!"

All the same, she eyed them doubtfully. "You can really eat these?"

Daisy bounced forward jauntily. "I'll try one if you will!"

Lucky watched as the giant dog and the little one crunched a beetle each. Their expressions of uncertainty gave way to a brightening of the eyes and a pricking of the ears.

"That's not bad at all," observed Daisy.

"Really rather nice!" said Martha, in a tone of elegant astonishment.

That was enough to reignite the whole Pack's enthusiasm. At Martha's recommendation, they all bounded off in search of rocks and branches and roots, and foraged beneath them.

This, Lucky decided some time later as Alfie pounced with delight on a green beetle, was a much better idea. It gave the dogs some practice in stalking, with a reward at the end of it – however much Sunshine wrinkled her little black nose. Even she was hungry enough, eventually, not to mind the taste and the crunch of spiders and insects, and Mickey in particular was getting the hang of slinking low along the ground, snuffling at the rough grass, then pouncing.

"Well, Bruno," said Martha with amusement as the bulldog chewed on a particularly plump spider. "Did you ever think we'd be doing this?"

"No indeed," he chuckled as he gulped it down. "No indeed!"

They'd come close to the edge of a belt of trees as they worked, and now Lucky sniffed the air. There would be larger prey in here, the kind that didn't disappear down holes. Squirrels, and birds, perhaps – even a nest full of eggs if they were lucky. Maybe they were ready for a bigger challenge. It was getting later in the day, and bugs only went so far towards filling hungry stomachs.

Mickey had come to his side with surprising quietness, and now he said hesitantly, "Lucky ... I've been thinking."

"What?"

The other dog looked a little awkward. "I know you're the expert, but ... these rabbits are so fast. I wondered ..." he looked at his paws "... suppose Bruno and Alfie go to the other side of the trees, downwind. And you and I and the others could drive out any game from here … let them smell us? Then when they run, they'll run right into –"

"Bruno and Alfie!" This was an inspired idea! Lucky was impressed. "It's worth a try. Come on, let's suggest it to the others."

Some of the dogs were doubtful, but Bruno and Alfie were more than willing to trot a cautious wide circle to the far side of the copse, and despite their ungainly-looking forms, managed to do it without too much noise and disturbance. These dogs, who he'd thought so spoiled and soft, were learning quickly. Three birds took frightened flight, clattering up through the branches, and a mouse scuttled into a hole in a tree trunk, but there was no mass stampede of prey. The Sun-Dog had bounded to his highest point in the sky; perhaps most small creatures were dozing now, sleepy with warmth.

Mickey was proving to be a natural. He slunk into the undergrowth, sniffing for possibilities, and though his first find was a squirrel that scurried out of reach up a pine trunk, he didn't waste time and energy barking at it. Daisy, overexcited by the prospect of meat at last, put her forepaws on the trunk and yapped, but even that was no disaster – alarmed into unwise flight, a rabbit bolted from the grass.

Mickey and Daisy were after it at once. Lucky had to force himself not to spring after it too – this was a challenge for the Leashed Dogs, not him. There was a slab of rock at the edge of the wood, and he leapt up on to it, watching the chase. The rabbit Daisy had scared scuttled into a hole, unreachable, but another instantly panicked and ran – straight towards the place where Bruno and Alfie were waiting. Lucky felt a flicker of excitement. *This might work!*

Bella and Mickey raced after the rabbit, and even Sunshine joined in. Little Daisy wasted energy barking her excitement – *Not again!* thought Lucky. *She needs to calm down!*

But just as Bruno and Alfie burst from the undergrowth ahead, forcing the rabbit to double back, it was Daisy who was in the right place. As the rabbit ran almost between her paws, she made a wild pounce-and-grab – and caught it!

It struggled so hard she'd have lost it straight away, except that the other dogs were on it in an instant. Martha slapped her big paws on to its back, holding it firmly, and Daisy gripped a hindleg desperately between her teeth. Now that it was immobile, Bruno grabbed it securely and finished it off with a shake of his powerful jaws.

For a moment they stood panting, staring at one another with delight.

"We did it!" squealed Sunshine.

"Well done, Daisy," rumbled Bruno, dropping the dead rabbit to the ground. "Well done!"

It wasn't enough to fill all their bellies, thought Lucky as he put a paw on the still-warm body and began to tear it into portions, but it was a start – and more than that, it had once again given him hope for the future. Mickey's instincts had been right back there – and that was further proof that the Leashed Dogs must still have some instincts left that could help them survive. Mickey's dog-spirit was waking inside him, and Mickey was listening to its voice. If all the dogs followed his example, they had a chance of becoming a true Pack – a free, wild Pack!

CHAPTER FIFTEEN

The hollow by the river was an excellent location to settle and make a proper camp. The place they'd slept last no-sun had been fine, but Lucky knew they needed to find a more permanent base, one that could protect them.

There was a broad stretch of grass protected both by the rising ground that stretched away from the river and by a tangled thicket of bush that would give shelter if it rained. With their hunger lessened somewhat by the rabbit and bugs they had eaten, the dogs could sit, heads cocked, and listen to the soothing trickle of water over stones, and watch the light play on the rippling surface.

"It's perfect," sighed Sunshine happily. "Who'd

have thought we'd find a new home so quickly!"

"And not too far from the longpaws," added Mickey. "We'll be able to go back to the city quite easily when they come back for us."

Lucky couldn't help giving a small growl of despair, but he managed to keep it to a muffled rumble in his throat. "Don't get too comfortable," he warned them. "We have to stay alert."

"Oh, nonsense," yapped Alfie. "Why would we ever move from here? It's so clever of you to find this place, Lucky!"

Best not to say any more, Lucky decided. Instead he gave a more cheerful bark. "The ground is good, but you'll soon feel every single pebble against your bones. Let's gather some leaves. It'll be much more comfortable than lying on grass."

The other dogs were enthusiastic enough not to grumble at this task, and they bounded energetically into the trees, seizing jawfuls of soft fallen leaves and bringing them back to scatter on the ground beneath the scrubby bush till there was a messy heap of them. Bella and Martha scraped the pile together into a good thick bed, broad enough for all of them if they lay snuggled close together.

Stepping back, Bella examined their work with

satisfaction, though Sunshine had now flopped down, panting.

"Being a wild dog is such hard work!"

Bella licked her ear. "And we haven't finished yet."

"Bella's right," Lucky agreed. "We have to organise ourselves. We all have different talents. Let's make use of them."

"I don't think I'm good at anything," said Sunshine mournfully, her ears drooping.

"That isn't true," said Lucky heartily. "You have sharp eyes and a good nose. You can patrol for dangers. You and Daisy!"

Daisy gave an excited yap. "Oh, yes! I can do that, Lucky!"

"You think I can do that?" Sunshine pricked her ears doubtfully. "All right, Lucky! I'll try my best. And I can look for more leaves ..."

Lucky felt his eyes twinkling with amusement. "I think we have enough of those at the moment, but you should keep an eye out for anything else we could use. Alfie could scout for that sort of thing, too. Mickey? You should be in charge of looking for food."

"Yes," agreed Bella. "Mickey's the best hunter. He should come with me."

Mickey positively swelled with pride, yelping

proudly through his mouthful of glove.

"And Bruno and Martha can stand guard?" Bella looked questioningly at Lucky.

"Yes! Martha, you'll be especially good at watching for trouble from the riverside."

Sitting around Lucky in a semicircle, the dogs gave him looks of pride and gratitude, and he found himself touched by their trust. He yelped encouragingly and pawed the ground. "Let's get started!"

Sunshine bounded after Lucky, along with Daisy and Alfie, as he trotted out of the makeshift camp.

"We could go back towards the field where we saw the longpaws," suggested Alfie. "What do you think, Lucky?"

At his side Daisy shivered nervously. "Maybe not exactly that direction," Lucky said, with a swift reassuring nuzzle at Daisy's head, "but we could take a wide circle around it. I don't want to run into any of those yellow longpaws again, but there might be things they've left behind, things we could use."

"Good idea!" yapped Alfie, and bounded ahead, up a shallow slope and on to the grassy plateau.

They weren't nearly as far from the city as Lucky would have liked, but there were advantages to being around old longpaw places. It wasn't long before they came in sight of a small wooden longpaw house that looked deserted, tucked between a rough field and a copse of trees. Was it a longpaw house – or something else?

Lucky sniffed the ground very carefully, but couldn't find a fresh scent. "Can you help, Sunshine?" She placed her yellow leash on the ground and the two of them worked together, their noses close to the earth, but they couldn't find any clues. "Let's have a look around," he murmured.

The four dogs edged nervously around a broken wire fence and began to explore. A scruffy-looking building leaned against the house like a longpaw who'd been drinking fire-juice. Pawing the splintered wooden door, Lucky felt it give abruptly, and he jumped back as it creaked and groaned and collapsed inwards.

Hackles high, they sniffed the dank air inside. There was a sharp smell of the liquid that longpaws gave to their loudcages to make them run, but the loudcage that squatted in the shack, apparently asleep, didn't look as if it had run anywhere for a long time. It was dented and rusty, and its round rubber paws were flat against the stone floor. Its big round eyes didn't flash, even when Lucky pushed the loudcage's door with a paw, and one of them was broken into sharp shards.

"This loudcage hasn't been used for a long time,' announced Daisy, proud of her knowledge.

"I don't think it'll howl …" said Lucky doubtfully.

"Of course it won't howl," said Sunshine. "It's dead."

Well, these dogs know more about longpaw things than I do, thought Lucky. He hesitantly pawed at the loudcage's door, but it didn't swing open for him the way the broken loudcage in the city had, when it let him sleep inside.

Alfie barked at a small bar of metal set into the door. "That bit. Pull that, Lucky!"

More determinedly Lucky scraped at the metal lever till he felt it give under his paw. As soon as she heard the loud *clunk,* Daisy grabbed the edge of the door with her teeth and pulled it wide.

Lucky gave her an admiring glance, then sniffed at the inside of the loudcage. "That was clever, Daisy."

She wagged her brown tail with pleasure. "Let's look inside!"

The loudcage smelled of old and acrid longpaw smoke. The tanned skin of its seats was torn and mouldy, and Lucky wrinkled his muzzle. Alfie, though, squeezed past him and began to tug at the skin with his teeth.

It must be dead, Lucky thought. *Otherwise it would definitely be wailing by now!*

When he was quite sure of that, Lucky joined Alfie in tearing at the skin till it was coming off in strips with an awful, but rather satisfying, ripping noise. "We can't eat this," he pointed out curiously.

"I have," said Alfie mischievously. "I've eaten it lots of times. It doesn't taste very good, but it's fun."

Sunshine gave a little giggling yelp of agreement. "My longpaw was so cross when I chewed hers!"

"I bet she didn't smack you," said Daisy.

"Of course not," said Sunshine smugly. "She never smacked me, but I didn't get a treat before bedtime. Still, it was worth it."

"The thing is," Daisy told Lucky, "this stuff is terribly comfy to lie on."

Lucky pricked his ears and wagged his tail hard, looking from face to face. "Well done!" he exclaimed proudly, and tore at the scat-skin with renewed enthusiasm.

"*And* there's a soft-hide in the back," pointed out Sunshine, putting her paws on the seat-back and panting eagerly as she peered over. "It doesn't look very clean, but it'll be cosy."

By the time they left the shack, they held in their jaws a magnificent haul of soft loudcage skin-strips and one tattered soft-hide. It was awkward carrying it all back to the camp, but even Sunshine didn't complain. Their reception from the rest of the Pack made the small dogs lift their heads and trot with pride.

"Daisy!" exclaimed Bella. "All of you! Where did you find those?"

It took Daisy and Sunshine a long time to tell the story, they were so breathless with excitement. While they explained their adventure, Lucky and Alfie were left to pull the soft-hide and the pieces of skin on to the leaf-bed. But Lucky didn't mind. *They're taking pride in their dog-spirit.*

Bella gazed admiringly at their new and splendid sleeping-place. "We had good luck too," she told Lucky. "Mickey found a squirrel, and we caught another rabbit!"

"That's wonderful." Lucky licked his litter-sister's muzzle. "Did you keep some for us?"

"We haven't even started it yet," she told him, mock-indignantly. "As if we would!"

Well, he thought to himself, *you haven't been really, truly hungry so far* ... But all he said was, "Thank you, Bella! That's good Pack work."

"And there's something else." She nipped gently at his nose. "Come and see what Martha found."

Bella led him over towards the river. Martha and Mickey were pawing energetically at a boulder on the banks of the stream, and Lucky and Bella had to wade into the water to watch them properly.

"Look!" Martha turned to him, panting. "Isn't this perfect?"

Lucky peered at the big flat rock, and saw straight away that of course they weren't trying to dig away at solid stone. Beneath the rock there was a small cavern formed by thick tree roots, and Mickey and Martha had hollowed it out. It now formed a deep hole beneath the bank, and the very edge of the stream rippled across its entrance. Martha gazed at Lucky expectantly as he explored it with his muzzle.

"We can keep extra food here – if we have any!" she told him. "It'll stay cool so it'll still taste good, and it won't go bad so quickly. Like a longpaw cold-box!"

Lucky stepped back into the stream, deeply impressed. "Martha, that's brilliant."

"Isn't it?" agreed Bella. "It was Martha and Mickey's idea." She sounded terribly proud of her Leashed friends' initiative. Although he doubted they'd ever have much food to spare, it was the kind of practical, longpaw-ish idea that would never have occurred to him.

As if reading his thoughts, Bella said, "I think we should try to keep a little food back whenever we can. It'll be difficult, but it'll mean we always have something to keep us going if – well, if we can't catch any food one sun-up, for instance."

"That's a smart idea," Lucky told her approvingly. "In the meantime we must all be hungry. Let's share Mickey and Bella's prey."

It was a popular suggestion, and the other dogs watched admiringly as Mickey and Bella divided up the rabbit and the squirrel, tugging them into bits of fur and flesh and nudging the pieces to their friends. As they worked, Lucky glanced at the sky, feeling the hairs on his back prickle. Things looked grey and bleak up there, as though the Sky-Dogs were getting ready for something. They should make their offering and eat quickly, Lucky decided. Then he hesitated.

"It's a long time since I shared my food with the Earth-Dog," he said, ashamed. "I've been so busy trying to survive, I haven't been able to spare even a scrap. She's brought me this far, and I have to give her some prey, too."

"But –" Bruno opened his jaws to protest as Lucky began to scrape a hole in the earth. He noticed Martha shoot Bruno a warning look.

Lucky picked up a rabbit leg in his teeth, and dropped it reverently into the hole. For a moment he closed his eyes, thanking the Earth-Dog, then scraped soil back over the chunk of flesh.

When he looked up, all the other dogs were staring at him, but at least they knew better than to say anything. *They'll learn.*

"Now," Lucky said, "we can eat!"

The rest of the dogs exchanged glances, their shoulders sagging with relief and their tongues flicking out to lick their chops as Lucky shared out the meat. When each dog had a chunk to gnaw on, there were two haunches left over, and Mickey put his paw on them.

"Let's put these in our cold-box. For tomorrow, just in case."

"Yes." Lucky paused in chewing at his tender piece of rabbit. Despite his approval of Mickey's forward planning, he felt a little tremor of distaste. "But can we call it our 'river-store' instead of a 'cold-box'?"

Bella gave an amused bark and licked his ear fondly. "Well, I don't see why not. That's a much better name anyway. More … more *doggish*."

"Yes," agreed Lucky, relieved. At that moment he felt something wet splash on to his ear, and he shook his head, only to feel two more cold spots on his skull and his other ear. "It's going to *pour –*"

Sure enough, they all raised their heads and heard the distant rumble of the Sky-Dogs growling, as the rain suddenly spattered harder on their hides. Sunshine crouched whimpering beneath Martha's flanks.

"Not thunder!" she whined.

"Another Sky-Dog fight." Lucky shivered. "It's time to test our shelter."

Together they crept on to the sleeping space beneath the tangled branches of the thorn bush, and huddled in a heap of warm bodies, Sunshine and Daisy tucked safely in the middle. Each of the dogs had pulled their longpaw things close beside them – Mickey settled beside his glove and Daisy rested a paw on her leather pouch. Lucky could feel Sunshine trembling against his flank, and the warmth of Bella's throat where she rested her head across his shoulders. The closeness, the strong beating hearts of other dogs, sent visions of the Pup-Pack flashing through his head again, but it no longer made him uneasy. Now, the memory was comforting.

The storm was over soon. Lucky raised his head as the sky lightened, and watched the black thundering cloudbank drift out over the distant ocean.

"You know what was happening, don't you?" Lucky said, almost to himself.

"No," Sunshine said, her voice full of misery. Lucky knew he could make her feel better if he shared a story. The little dog edged out slightly so that she could train her eyes on Lucky's face.

"The Sky-Dogs sent out Lightning, to tease the Earth-Dog. But the Sun-Dog growled his displeasure – they were the rolls of thunder – and sent the Sky-Dogs and Lightning packing. Now, the Sun-Dog blazes once more and the wet leaves glitter. See?"

Hesitantly Lucky crept across the shivering bodies of the other dogs and nosed the air. It still tasted of battle and lightning, but the sky was clear and bright once more.

Lucky glanced back at the others' nervous and expectant faces. A few drops of rain had leaked through to their sleeping-place, but the overhanging bush had protected them all remarkably well. Lucky barked happily.

"Come on! It's fresh water from the Sky-Dogs!"

He bounded into the open, where a puddle of new rain glinted in the hollow. He leapt wildly into it, and Bruno and Mickey followed on his heels, rolling and barking with glee. The rest were quick to join them.

The clear puddle was soon a splattered patch of mud, and their legs and bellies were black with it; Sunshine was the first to escape the puddle, trot towards the river and splash delicately into the calm eddying pool at its edge, letting the water wash her white fur. When they'd all swum themselves clean – Bruno with some trepidation, though Martha stayed protectively close to him – they clambered from the stream and shook themselves dry. Each dog, Lucky realised, was thoroughly wetting the others with every shake, the scattering showers of water glinting in the sun-high light.

Panting, he flopped on to the flat rock at the edge of the river and watched Mickey roll blissfully in the dry sand on the shore. The Sun-Dog's rays were deliciously warm on his heaving flanks, and Bella soon came to join him, followed by the others. Only Martha still stood in the river, lapping at the water, enjoying its flow around her legs.

Sunshine was right, he realised. *It really is perfect here.*

Carefully he licked his paws. Perhaps, soon, they would take him bounding across open land again ...

But he couldn't think about leaving the others, not yet. These dogs were getting better at listening to their dog-spirits – so much better – but they had a long way to go. When they could look after themselves, when they could hunt and survive and thrive alone: *that* would be the time for Lucky to leave.

CHAPTER SIXTEEN

"Look! Look what I *caught!*"

Lucky opened one eye and pricked an ear. It had been his waking routine for the last several days. The late sun-high was warm and humming with bees, and he was almost too comfortable to move. But Daisy loved to impress him; sleepily he wondered what she'd brought him this time. It was hard work feigning enthusiasm over her latest beetle, but he was fond of the young dog and he didn't want to disappoint her, so he hauled himself to his feet and sniffed eagerly as she came bounding towards him.

At his forepaws, she dropped the prey. It was a good bit larger – and furrier – than a beetle.

"A mole? That's terrific!" Lucky licked her nose admiringly, and sniffed delicately at the tiny prey's big flat paws. They could tunnel so fast, these silky black creatures, burrowing swiftly out of reach when a dog had barely started to dig. Why, he'd only ever caught two of them himself, in his entire hunting life!

Daisy was swelling with pride, her tail thrashing furiously, as Bella, Bruno, Alfie and Martha gathered around to admire her catch.

"Daisy, that's wonderful!" said Bella. "I've never caught a mole!"

Lucky exchanged an affectionate glance with his litter-sister. She knew how important it was to encourage a dog like Daisy, barely more than a pup and so excited to learn. Bella had a great deal of good sense and instinct, thought Lucky warmly. She would be a good leader once he had moved on.

They were getting more organised as a group, and that made Lucky even more hopeful that they would thrive in the wild. In the last few days, he had stepped back a pace to let Mickey gain some leadership experience. With the herding dog in charge and Lucky supervising, all the Leashed Dogs' hunting skills had begun to improve. Working together, herding prey towards two or three of the Pack, they'd caught a few more rabbits and even a squirrel. It was enough to keep the hunger pangs at bay, together with bugs and grubs and the remains of a deer carcass – an old deer, Lucky reckoned, that must have died of weakness and exhaustion rather than a longpaw loudstick. Even Sunshine had developed a taste for raw wild meat. They'd be able to look after themselves soon.

But niggling at the back of Lucky's mind was always the horrible echo of his bad dreams. If something bad was coming, the Leashed Dogs had to be as ready as he was.

Lucky put a paw on the mole and let Daisy divide it with her teeth. *Earlier on in our journey,* he thought with pride, *she could never have done that!*

There was barely a nibble for each of the dogs, but Daisy solemnly nudged the biggest piece to Lucky with her nose.

"I don't know where we'd be without you, Lucky. I can hunt now!"

"You certainly can," agreed Bella solemnly. "It'll be a rabbit next, you'll see."

"Yes!" yipped Daisy, and turned, about to race off in search of one. But the party was interrupted by a sudden volley of high-pitched barking.

Their heads turned towards the sound, hackles raised and ears pricked forward. Lucky recognised the voice even before Martha barked, "That's Sunshine!"

Sure enough, the little dog raced through the trees and came to a skidding halt beside them. She was panting with exertion and panic, but she managed to gasp, "Mickey! Mickey's trapped!"

"Calm down, Sunshine!" yelped Bella. "What do you mean, trapped?"

"His collar – oh, please come, Bella. He's choking!"

Lucky sprang towards the trees, the other dogs at his heels, and let Sunshine lead them through a shallow glade and into a thick undergrowth of thorns and tangled branches.

"Here! He's here!" Sunshine pawed at the scrub.

Mickey's nose was sticking out through leaves, and now Lucky could see his eyes in the shadows, filled with fear, wide enough to show the whites. His tongue hung from his jaws as he tried to rasp air into his lungs.

"Don't move, Mickey!" Lucky barked urgently. He tried to rake aside the thick branches, stinging his paw pads on thorns. The others gathered behind him, not crowding around and panicking as they usually did but with eerie worried calm. They were giving Mickey and Lucky some space, but they couldn't help barking some rather useless advice, too.

"Pull him, Lucky!"

"Bite the branches off!"

Sunshine scraped the ground nervously with her front paws. "Oh, Lucky, please help him. He was only teaching me to hunt. I'm so hopeless and he's been so good..."

"I'm trying, Sunshine, hush! Bella, I need your help!"

She was at his side in an instant. "What do you want me to do, Lucky?"

He was thinking fast. Mickey didn't have long, if they couldn't stop that collar from choking him. He was trapped tightly by the thicket of thorns, and he couldn't seem to move forward at all, but perhaps...

"Here, Bella, your head is narrower than mine. Can you get a hold of his collar?"

Bella nudged and forced her way into the bushes, getting scratches on her muzzle and ears, but she managed to take Mickey's collar carefully between her teeth.

"Hold still! That's it – now, Mickey, you have to go backwards."

Mickey looked up at Lucky with frightened eyes. "Backwards?' he gasped. "*Deeper* into the thorns?"

"Yes. Wriggle backwards. Trust me!"

Mickey only needed to be told once. Lucky just wished he could be as sure as Mickey that he knew what he was doing…

Planting his forepaws as well as he could on the ground, the dog wriggled and shoved desperately backwards, flinching as the thorns dug harder into his hide. But the branches were giving, gradually. Despite Mickey's awkward struggles, Bella managed to keep a tight hold of his collar, her paws scrabbling for purchase on the sandy soil.

"That's it! Well done," cried Lucky. "Just a little more, Mickey. Turn your head – Bella, *pull!*"

Mickey shot backwards into the bush, yelping as the prickles caught his haunches. But the collar was off, dangling loose in Bella's jaws, and it took him no time to scramble free of the thorn bush. The others clustered around him, yipping their relief and delight.

Sunshine bounced on her hindpaws, licking Mickey's jaws. "Mickey, you're all right! Oh, thank you, Lucky. I *knew* you'd be able to do it."

"Mickey and Bella did most of it," Lucky pointed out. "Mickey, are you hurt?"

Mickey stood squarely and gave himself a violent shake, sending twigs and leaves flying. "Just a few scratches. I'm sorry, Lucky, that was stupid of me."

"It could happen to any of us," Lucky consoled him, adding dryly, "Those of us wearing a collar, anyway."

"My collar!" Mickey started. Glancing left to right, he caught sight of the brown leather strap, still gripped in Bella's mouth. Mickey licked her nose gratefully. "There it is. And it isn't even broken!"

Lucky couldn't believe his eyes as Bruno padded up and took the other side of the collar in his jaws, so he and Bella were holding it between them, stretching it out to its full extent. Mickey shoved his nose into it and tried to wriggle back in.

"What are you *doing?*"

Bruno gave him a surprised look. "Helping, of course."

"Helping him do what?" Lucky sat down on his haunches, flummoxed. "Put it back *on?*"

"Of course." Mickey gave him a nervous glance, while Bella looked a little apologetic. "It's my collar. Why wouldn't I wear it?"

"Because of what just happened!" barked Lucky in exasperation. "If we hadn't been here, you'd have been strangled!"

"But you *were* here," pointed out Mickey reasonably.

Lucky raised his head and barked angrily at the sky. "You should get rid of those collars altogether! They can trap you, choke you. And if you ever got into a fight with some other dog – well, you wouldn't have a chance!"

"That's not true!" snapped Bruno. Proudly he squared his shoulders and jutted his head forward. "Not have a chance? I've got the blood of fighting dogs in me! My collar doesn't change that!"

"Bruno's right," yelped Sunshine, and the others barked in agreement.

Lucky's temper flared, lifting his hackles on his back and curling the skin of his muzzle. These dogs were making him crazy – one minute, they showed all the instincts necessary to live and thrive in this broken world; the next they were behaving like puppies, pining for their longpaws' restraints.

"I'll prove it to you!" Lucky growled, charging at Bruno. The bulldog was so startled he flinched back, and in that moment Lucky seized his thick leather collar between his jaws. Bruno fought to keep his balance, but it was no use; he was dragged over by Lucky, who twisted his neck, flinging the other dog around. Bruno was heavy and thickset, but it was easy for Lucky to use the collar to gain leverage and throw him sideways.

The rest of the dogs were barking in protest and fear now, and Bruno was yelping, trying to fight back but unable to get leverage with his paws. Lucky shook him like a huge trapped squirrel.

"Oh, Lucky, please!" cried Daisy above the scared

racket of the others. "Please don't hurt him!"

Lucky released Bruno, and let him flop to the ground, panting for breath. He put a paw on the bulldog's chest; that was too much for Bruno, who rolled over with a growl and staggered to his feet, then shook himself from head to tail. Lucky returned his glare, and it wasn't long before Bruno dropped his eyes.

"You see?" said Lucky. "Do you see now?" He kept his voice low and averted his eyes from the bulldog's to prove the fight was over. He felt guilt prickling under his fur. He'd worked out all his temper on poor, gutsy Bruno. *I shouldn't have done that …*

But they *had* to learn, and he was the only teacher they had. "You see how vulnerable a collar makes you? I bet Bruno could beat me in a fair fight," he said, with a glance at the stocky dog, "but with his collar on, I could do what I liked. Trust me. You should take them off."

The Pack exchanged shocked glances, and one or two of them stared at their paws. It was little Daisy who finally summoned up the nerve to answer him.

"Lucky," she whined softly, "I know how you feel about this. We all do. But – but my collar? I can't take it off. *I won't*. I'll do anything else you ask me, but please don't ask me that. It shows I'm bound to a longpaw, that I'm owned and loved and that I have a longpaw to look after. It's so important. To *all* of us."

Lucky stared at her, bewildered at such a long, firm speech from this pup.

"But Daisy," he said, "you don't have a longpaw now. They're gone."

She whimpered and averted her eyes.

"I don't care if I don't have longpaws just now," Mickey said. His dark eyes met Lucky's, respectful but determined. "I'll find them again. If I have to learn to fight better, that's what I'll do – but I will put my collar back on. I won't give up on my longpaws."

Lucky realised he was wasting his breath. He turned and padded away over the beaten earth and back towards their camp. He couldn't bear to watch as Sunshine and Martha joined in the efforts to replace Mickey's collar.

He heard the sound of paws behind him, and glanced over his shoulder. There was Bella, her eyes beseeching.

"Lucky, you have to try to understand. Collars are important to us. They're part of who we are."

They're part of who you've been made to be, he wanted to say. But there was no arguing with his litter-sister at the moment, so he kept quiet, shaking himself and padding on.

A distant yelping and whining startled him. *Alfie!*

Lucky picked up speed and turned towards the sound of his barks, but realised with relief that they weren't the cries of danger and distress – Alfie just couldn't find the Pack.

"Everyone? Bella! Lucky, Bruno! Where *are* yooooou?"

Bella was behind him as he trotted back into the camp, and he could hear the rest following behind in a racket of broken twigs and scattering stones. Hunting-craft was all but forgotten for today, then.

When Alfie caught sight of them emerging from the trees, the short, squat little dog bounded across to them with delight, yapping his welcome, oblivious to the recent frictions. *Every dog has something to bring to the Pack,* Lucky thought. They were lucky to have a dog like Alfie to lighten tense moments.

"You're here! I thought you'd forgotten me!"

"As if we could," barked Bella in amusement as he jumped to lick her nose. "Did you have any luck with hunting?"

"No." Alfie's ears drooped, but only for a moment; then he was dancing on his paws once more. "But I found something else!"

"What?" asked Martha, pricking her ears.

"Tell us!" yelped Daisy, clearly relieved to have a

distraction from the quarrel.

Alfie sat back and scratched at his ear. Lucky could see he was delighted to have a story to tell and determined to make the most of it. "I walked a long way. All on my own. I like to be alone sometimes," he added with a glance at Lucky as if seeking approval. "I investigated the little valley, there – and those hills. I even went beyond them!"

Lucky was startled. The valley that sloped gently away from the grassland, up beyond the trees, was quite broad, and the hills beyond it were rocky and steep. He'd investigated the area a little himself, on one of the nights he had prowled the territory checking for danger, but he certainly hadn't gone beyond the hills. The squat dog must have explored a long way.

"That could have been dangerous, Alfie," Lucky chided him gently, though he could relate more than ever to Alfie's need to be alone. "But what did you find?"

"Dogs!" he announced triumphantly. "Lots of *dogs!*"

The others yapped and barked at the news, and Daisy performed her spinning-a-circle trick, bouncing with excitement. "What were they like, Alfie?" she yelped. "Are they friendly? Can they help us?"

"I don't know. I didn't go that far. But I heard them! And I smelled them too – and there was something else!"

Lucky's skin prickled with unease, but the others were too excited to worry.

"What?" yipped Sunshine. "What was it?"

Alfie's eyes gleamed. "Food. Lots and *lots* of food!"

CHAPTER SEVENTEEN

"Let's go," yapped Sunshine. "Let's go there now and introduce ourselves!"

"That's a wonderful idea," said Mickey warmly.

Lucky took a breath as the others barked and yelped with the eagerness to investigate. He was uncomfortably aware that the questions he was about to ask could cause another squabble. "Alfie, what kind of dogs were they?"

"I don't know. They were dogs! Like us! But with food!"

"Not all dogs are like us. What if they're hostile? What if it's a Wild Pack? They'll defend their territory if they are. You shouldn't mess with a Wild Pack – and they won't choose to share food with you."

Sunshine was crestfallen, but Bruno interrupted. "There's no harm in looking."

"There could be plenty of harm in it," growled Lucky. "I don't like this. I'm sorry. It sounds dangerous."

"Oh, Lucky," yipped Bella fondly. "You think everything is dangerous! You're a wonderful leader, but perhaps you should stop being quite so cautious."

"If there's food for the taking, we can't *not* look," added Bruno. "This could mean we wouldn't have to tire ourselves out by hunting!"

Lucky realised the bulldog was still aggrieved about the fight demonstration. He sighed. "We don't know anything about these dogs," he protested.

"But we can find out. The least we can do is look," suggested Martha.

"I agree," Bruno said.

"And if they're smaller than us," said Bella, throwing Lucky a challenging glare, "there won't be a problem."

"Bella's right," put in Mickey. "Why don't we at least go and investigate?"

"It would be easier than hunting beetles," said Sunshine mournfully, sitting down and tapping the ground with her tail.

What's wrong with beetles all of a sudden? Lucky pawed at one that was clambering over a grass stem, but he'd lost his appetite. He didn't like the way Bella was looking at him: she was drawn up to her full height and her ears were turned back, almost as if she was spoiling for a fight. When a squirrel in one of the treetops chirruped angrily at them, she didn't even flick an ear; she just went on staring at Lucky with her head slightly tilted.

"Tell you what," Bella suggested. "Some of us can go and investigate. The rest will stay here, as a sort of backup team, and to guard the camp while we're gone. A small group will be less noticeable anyway. I'd suggest me, Daisy, Alfie and Lucky."

Lucky studied the hopeful eyes and the pricked ears of the little group. *I have a bad feeling about this,* Lucky thought. But he knew that if he was going to leave these dogs to cope on their own one day, they had to start making their own decisions – and he had to trust them. "All right. But at the first sign of trouble – turn tails! The rest of you, stay close to the camp."

Whatever happened next, Lucky would just have to be ready.

***

Alfie seemed happy to be lead dog for a change.

He'd found a path through the brush, beaten down by small animals, and there was plenty of shade dappling the way, at least till they reached the beginning of the slope. As they stepped out from beneath tree cover, the late Sun-Dog's rays beat down on them, and by the time they'd climbed to the ridge they were all moving sluggishly. When Alfie paused in the shadow of a tree even Lucky flopped down.

"We should rest," he told them.

"It's not far now," panted Alfie, still eager.

"We'll get moving again soon," promised Bella, wagging her tail. "When I say so, be ready to go."

She'd raised her voice to be sure it would reach Lucky. He laid his head on his paws and turned away, glaring down into the valley. She was making sure her so-called Pack knew who was boss, that was all.

Let her! It's not as if they're my Pack!

Lucky followed Alfie as he led them down a winding rabbit-path. His mind was a tumble of conflict and uncertainty. How would a Wild Pack react to the approach of a bunch of Leashed Dogs? Would they be driven off with their tails between their legs? How would Bella's leadership skills stand up if she had to talk her way out of a fight?

Suddenly Alfie squeaked: "There. Look!"

Lucky halted with the others and sniffed the air doubtfully. Yes, he could scent them – dogs, a good many of them – and he was fairly sure he didn't like it. The scent was dark, bitter and musky, and it reeked of anger – not that it seemed to bother the others. From the shade of a small scrubby tree, they gazed out at the scene below.

The valley was broad and dotted with longpaw buildings; but these longpaw buildings didn't look like the longpaw homes that Lucky had seen in the city. They were too short, for one thing. In fact, their doors looked dog-sized. The walls were plain, and the windows had metal bars across the holes where most longpaw buildings had clear-stone. They seemed less damaged than the buildings in the city, but there were a few vicious cracks running up some of the walls.

There was something unnatural about the sight, something frightening that would have made Lucky want to run away as fast as he could in any direction – if it hadn't been for the scent of food.

It was a strong, tantalizing odour. Not longpaw food like the Food House owner had given him, Lucky decided – but very definitely food made of meat. Lucky felt his mouth water and licked his chops. His stomach grumbled. There was no sign of movement below – not that that made Lucky feel any better.

So where were the dogs he could smell? Lucky's heartbeat quickened. He'd worked so hard to look after the Pack, and he couldn't put them in danger now. But his stomach was telling him something different. If these were friendly dogs – friends with food … perhaps Bella was right and they would share what they had. It had to be worth exploring.

"All right," he said slowly. "Let's go closer. Stick together and try not to draw attention to yourselves. Not until we know what type of dogs are down there."

Creeping forwards, then running low, they scampered towards the fence and peered through. Bella put her forepaws up against the wire, snuffling.

"Look," she breathed in awe. "Look at all that food!"

In front of the low houses there were metal bowls, some with a thin puddle of water in them, some brim-full of dry-looking nuggets of meat. Once again Lucky licked saliva from his jaws. It wasn't like live rabbit, but it did smell good. And there was so much of it …

"I think it's …" whispered Alfie haltingly. "It *smells* like …"

"Like our home-food,' agreed Bella in a murmur. "It's like the food the longpaws used to give us."

"Oh …" Daisy breathed a nostalgic, hungry sigh. "I'd love to taste that again …"

Even as they watched, they heard a loud click. All the dogs froze, limbs stiffening and muscles tensing to run, but no one appeared, longpaw or dog. Instead, more of those nuggets poured from holes in the wall into the metal bowls, making some of them overflow, and fresh clear water streamed into every second bowl.

It was too much for Bella. She hopped on her hind paws, sticking her nose desperately through the wire, whining and scratching at the fence with her claws.

"It's amazing! Food that comes from nowhere! We *have* to get in!"

Lucky cocked his head, staring at the bowls, as the others nuzzled and poked their noses under the fence, searching for gaps and scraping at the earth. Certainly it seemed quiet enough, he thought.

So why was the dog-spirit inside him telling him to run?

"Here!" yelped Alfie. "I've found a hole!"

The others bounded towards it, but Lucky approached more cautiously, watching the dark entrance to the closest building for any sign of movement.

He could smell dogs, and he could see their food. So where were they?

His hackles bristled, and he took a pace back. The Leashed Dogs were surviving on the food they hunted;

did they really need these overflowing bowls of extra food?

"Lucky, come and see!" cried Daisy. "I can dig deeper. Just you watch – I'll make us a way in!"

"No." Lucky shook his head. "This doesn't feel right. There's danger here. Can't you sense it? We should get away while we can. You can hunt now – we don't need others to give us our food."

"Don't be silly,' snapped Bella. "Why should we hunt, when all this is here for the taking?"

Lucky's skin prickled all over as he looked at the late Sun-Dog glinting off the shiny metal bowls. "That's the point. Don't you see how much food there is? How big those bowls are? How big do you think the dogs are that live here? Do you think you'd win a fight? We haven't seen them, but why? Are they hiding?"

Daisy glanced nervously at Bella, but the bigger dog growled, "We can look after ourselves."

Lucky whined. Every moment he spent in this place made him more uneasy. He was wrong to have let the Pack come here. The sensation in his hide had become a tingling, almost unbearable sense of threat, similar to the way he felt before a Sky-Dog battle – or before the Big Growl shattered the world. And worse, it was waking the memory of his terrible dreams: the dreams that didn't make sense. The *Storm of Dogs* ...

They had to get out of here.

"Please, Bella!" he started to say.

Springing up on to a higher hillock of earth by the fence, Bella snarled. "That's it! *I'm* the Alpha of this Pack, Lucky. I brought you in. You might be very clever on your own, but this is *our* kind of place. And I say we're going in!"

Lucky bared his teeth at her. "Stop acting like a spoiled puppy! You've no idea what being an Alpha is all about!"

"Oh, and you do?" Legs stiff, hackles high, Bella stalked round him, growling. "We were doing just fine before we met you. You're the one who's showing off. Pretending you know it all!"

"I know a lot more than you do, Leashed Dog!" snarled Lucky. "You don't know anything about staying alive! You're all soft, and you've got no sense. No – no *dog-spirit!*" That was about as bad an insult as he could find to throw at her. Guilt plunged through him, but it wasn't enough to overwhelm his anger. *How dare she! After everything I've done for her!*

There was something else in Lucky's heart, too: a fear that pounded through him with every breath. These dogs looked up to Lucky as a leader, because he knew the lie of the land and could teach them crafty survival tricks. But it did not matter how crafty Lucky was, he knew what happened to dogs who lost challenges. He had seen it happen before. It was like their dog-spirit had been slashed, wounds ripped open and their essence, their bravery, their courage all seeped out. A defeated dog would duck his head in the presence of others, and keep his tail low, limp between his legs.

Lucky's instincts urged him to fight against this.

Bella barked in anger. "You talk a lot of nonsense!"

"Dog-spirit is what's inside us all," he snarled. "Or it should be! That's what protects us – along with the Sky-Dogs and the Forest-Dog and – oh, why am I bothering with you? You don't understand any of it!"

"Well, your so-called dog-spirit is making you a coward, Lucky!" growled Bella. Her lips were pulled back from her teeth as they circled each other. Alfie and Daisy watched fearfully, tails tucked firmly between their legs. "There aren't any other dogs here! Worse, there aren't any longpaws, either."

Lucky shivered with anger and frustration. He thought of the Fierce Dog who'd driven him away from the fire-box. Had Bella ever had to face a dog like that? Of course she hadn't – because she'd been protected by longpaws all her life. "There are dogs here! I can't see them, but I can smell them!"

"You can smell dogs that used to be here, maybe. It doesn't matter. I'm in charge, and I say we go in!"

Lucky gave a bitter snarl, and snapped the air. "You may be in charge of these *Leashed Dogs!* But you're not in charge of me, *Squeak,* and you never will be!"

Alfie gave a groan of protest, and Daisy whined, but Bella and Lucky ignored them. Lucky knew their barks were getting loud, but he no longer cared. He half-hoped they *would* be overheard and chased away from here before Bella did something stupid.

"I order you, Lucky!" she yelped. "I order you to come with us!"

"You can order all you like." Lucky curled his muzzle and sat down, scratching his ear with casual disdain. "You're not my Alpha. I'm not coming."

Daisy gasped.

"I'm the Alpha of this Pack!" barked Bella.

"And you're welcome to it!" He gave her a furious bark.

Bella fell silent, flanks heaving, saliva dripping from her jaws.

"Be that way, and see where it gets you, Lone Dog." Turning, she stalked off along the side of the fence, tail high. "You're not as smart as you think you are. There won't be any food for dogs who won't help get it!"

He shook his head in disbelief as she squirmed under the fence, followed by Alfie, They paced away towards the low houses. Daisy gave Lucky a mournful glance of longing, but she'd obviously taken Bella's declaration seriously.

"I'm sorry, Lucky," she said, then wriggled through the fence after them.

He watched the three dogs trot away, his heart pounding harder with every step they took towards those food bowls, until he couldn't watch any more. He walked a little distance back, then turned and lay down with his head on his paws, heaving an unhappy sigh.

They were in danger. He was sure of it. At every snap of a twig, every cry of a bird, his ears twitched and he lifted his head.

He couldn't leave them. Bella was his litter-sister; he owed it to her to see that she was safe – and she wasn't safe here. Maybe his fears were just the result of his solitary life, when he had to be alert for danger at every turn. On the other hand, he felt certain there was something deeply bad here, however much it seemed like a perfect place for a new camp. He could smell it in the air.

Slowly, he climbed to his feet.

Oh, Sky-Dogs, he thought to himself, *I hope I'm not making a stupid mistake …*

Turning back towards the strange Dog-Garden, he headed for the hole in the fence.

CHAPTER EIGHTEEN

Daisy had done a good job of scraping out the earth, and once Lucky forced his shoulders through, his haunches followed easily.

Once he was on the other side he paused, crouched against the ground, seeking some clue as to the whereabouts of the unfamiliar dogs that he could smell. Were they really gone? Perhaps they'd escaped in the Big Growl, or crawled through the gap under the fence. Maybe they'd preferred the freedom of the wild to the easy source of food.

A crow flapped into the air with a raucous caw, making Lucky jump with alarm. As his heart calmed he watched it as it settled on a branch, cocking its beady black eye at him.

The grass inside the compound was lush and green, cropped neatly short. *Longpaw work,* Lucky thought. Were there longpaws still alive here? He could smell nothing but dog. Beyond the grass loomed the dark shadow of the central big house, and Lucky narrowed his eyes in Sun-Dog's dying light, trying to make out what might lurk there.

He could see almost nothing from his position near the fence, and he knew with a lurching sense of fear that he was going to have to move further in. He couldn't make sure the others were all right if he stayed where he was. Gathering his courage, he set off, slinking so low to the ground his belly almost scraped the grass. He picked up speed and made it to a tree with spreading branches. It wasn't the best cover, but it would have to do.

He could see the others now, right in the shadow of the dog-houses. They weren't even trying to be quiet. Lucky's heart lurched with fear and anger. They weren't even trying to be careful. All three of them were wolfing down the food in the nearest bowls, and no one was keeping watch.

"It's delicious!" squeaked Daisy through a mouthful of nuggets.

"Mmmph," was all Alfie could reply for a moment.

Then he gave a loud yip of pure excitement, and plunged his muzzle back into the bowl.

Bella gulped down a half-crunched mouthful. "We must try to take some back for the others," Lucky heard her announce. "Maybe I'll even take some back for Lucky," she added haughtily.

Lucky's spine tingled with resentment. He'd only been trying to keep them safe. Still, it was hard to watch the others gorging themselves while he could only look on, his belly growling. Lucky looked around. Nothing – no sign of dogs or longpaws. *Were they right?* he thought. *Was I too cautious? Bella will be very smug if I admit it, but* ... Lucky began to slink forward.

And froze.

Around the corner of the biggest house stalked a group of sleek, ferocious-looking dogs.

Lucky's fur stood on end. He'd seen their kind before: dark lean bodies, pricked ears, pointed snouts that were bared more often than not in a snarl. He'd come across these dogs as guardians of longpaw homes and work-houses, doing the bidding of longpaws with harsh voices and glowing light-beams and vicious sticks.

Lucky backed swiftly behind the tree. They hadn't seen or scented him – their attention was focused on the others. At the clatter of paws on gravel, Alfie, Daisy and

Bella stopped gobbling and raised their heads in alarm; the fierce Pack had come from downwind, and had approached unnoticed. Now the big dogs spread out in a frighteningly disciplined circle, trapping the Leashed Dogs.

Bella and Alfie exchanged anxious glances. Daisy did the smartest thing in the circumstances, and rolled on to her back, whimpering as she exposed her throat and belly. *Good, Daisy!* thought Lucky, impressed. *That was quick thinking – and sensible.*

Alfie gave Daisy a nervous look and then followed her example, submitting to the other dogs. But Bella, stiff-legged and proud, curled her muzzle defiantly at the huge dogs.

Panic chilled Lucky's body, making breathing hard and sending his hackles bristling. *No, Bella! Don't be stupid. You don't stand a chance!*

He wanted to dash from the shelter of the tree, take her by the scruff of the neck and shake some sense into her. *She's so puffed with arrogance now that she's decided she's the Alpha,* he thought. *Please, Bella, don't be reckless.* His muscles trembled with the effort of not rushing to her side. But there was nothing he could do …

"You dare defy us?" One of the Fierce Dogs finally spoke, in a low vicious sneer. He sounded rather pleased that she was going to resist. The attack-dogs started to close their circle around Lucky's friends.

It was Daisy who came to Bella's rescue, whimpering desperately. "Bella. Please?"

Bella gave a small yip that told her to be quiet, but after a few moments she took a breath and dipped her head in defeat. As if it cost her a huge effort, she lay down awkwardly, submitting with the others.

Briefly Lucky closed his eyes, letting relief flood his limbs. He opened his eyes again to see that the Fierce Dogs had relaxed a little, pricking their ears and growling their approval. Thank the Sky-Dogs, Bella had come to her senses in time.

"How did you get in here?" The biggest and sleekest of the Fierce Dogs growled. Her voice was dark and deadly. She must be their Alpha, Lucky decided. Her legs and body were powerful with sinewy muscle and the others lowered their heads as she spoke, deferring to her. The evening light made her coat gleam.

Lucky watched the Leashed Dogs exchange glances, and for a moment the frightened Daisy seemed about to blurt a reply. But Bella interrupted.

"We jumped," she told the bigger dog, her bark nervous but quite steady. "Over the fence."

Lucky wanted to put his paws over his eyes. How

could she imagine the Fierce Dogs would fall for that one? As soon as they compared Daisy with the height of the fence, Bella was in for a sharp bite at best …

But perhaps the Fierce Dogs' brains weren't quite as sharp as their teeth, because the Alpha nodded slowly, still growling in her throat.

A big male snarled at Bella. "Steal our rations, would you? Impudent rats."

"Indeed." The Alpha peeled her lips back from her teeth, showing how deadly they were. "You're our prisoners now. And you will be until we decide what to do with you. Mace? Bring them."

The male dog opened his jaws and barked. It was the loudest, most threatening sound Lucky had ever heard from a dog, making him cower in his hiding place, and he wasn't surprised when Bella, Alfie and Daisy huddled obediently together and ducked their heads. Trembling, the Leashed Dogs were herded by the Fierce Dogs towards the big house, the bigger dogs occasionally snapping at their paws and tails. Daisy yelped with fright, and one of the Fierce Dogs loomed over her, barking and snapping his teeth in her face.

"Quiet! Keep moving!"

Daisy scurried on, tail between her hindlegs and ears drooping miserably. Alfie made a brave attempt to stay protectively at her side, but at a warning snarl he licked her ear and dropped reluctantly back.

Oh, Earth-Dog, who are these Fierce Dogs? wondered Lucky unhappily. The powerful black dogs were so ferocious, so unfriendly. They would surely shred the Leashed Dogs without much effort.

Please, Earth-Dog, Lucky willed. *Don't let Bella and the others die here. They were foolish, but they didn't mean any harm. They will learn. Let them get free …*

He had to get closer to the big house. If he was quick, he could make it while the black dogs' backs were turned. After that? Well … he'd just have to take his chances.

None of the Fierce Dogs glanced back, too busy watching their prisoners with glinting eyes, and Lucky seized the moment. Now! He darted out from the cover of the tree. *Quickly!* Crossing the horribly open space in the waning daylight seemed to take forever, but at last he scurried close to a cracked wall and slunk into its shadow.

Breathing more easily, Lucky panted his relief, and crept forward, keeping the group of dogs just in sight. He couldn't even see the Leashed Dogs now; the guard-dogs were packed tightly around them. His hide prickled with heat and fear, and his fur stood up all over his body, but he was still protected by the wall when he saw the Fierce

Dogs herd the others through a door in the side of the big house. Its walls were cracked in several places, but it looked solid and strong enough to hold them till the end of the world, when the Sky-Dogs would fall to earth.

It was hopeless. Lucky felt his tail droop, and his head dip as if a longpaw hand was forcing him to sniff the earth. His fear for the Leashed Dog Pack mixed with his sense of resentment at finding himself caught up in other dogs' problems. This was why he didn't want to be in a Pack – too many dogs couldn't move quickly. Too many dogs could get into trouble. A Pack Dog was responsible for his Packmates. A Lone Dog only had to rely on himself.

Sitting down to rest, but not daring to scratch his bristling neck fur, Lucky peered cautiously round the corner of the wall.

This is the best chance I'll have to get clear.

It made sense. All he could do now was save his own fur. Every instinct was telling him to run, quickly, while he still had the chance, and get as far from this sinister place as possible. There was nothing he could do to help dogs trapped in such a forbidding prison and guarded by hostile and deadly enemies. They should have listened to him before.

And yet ... he thought as he half-turned to go.

They are my friends …

He thought of the challenges they'd faced together, the small everyday achievements as they learnt to fend for themselves. He thought of Daisy's mole, and her pride and pleasure as she'd presented it to him. The way that Martha had launched herself into the river to rescue her friend. How Mickey had helped to herd his friends out of the city.

Lucky's decision was made.

He pressed close to the wall as he rounded the end of it, then raced across the last stretch of open ground. Blood thundering in his veins, he huddled against the wall beneath a barred, cracked window, panting as quietly as he could. He couldn't let the Fierce Dogs smell him, or hear his thrashing heart.

Then, for an instant, he thought his heart had stopped. The Alpha Fierce Dog, her voice as silky as it was vicious, was growling at her captives.

"Where is the other dog?"

Lucky's blood ran cold, and his skin tightened. The *other* dog?

He heard Bella's submissive whine, her frightened protestation. But the Alpha wasn't interested in denial. "You know very well, Pet Dog. The one like you. *Where is he?*"

"I don't know who you mean ..." whined Bella, then gave a yelp of shock as jaws snapped audibly.

"Oh yes, you do ..." snarled another Fierce Dog.

Lucky, listening beneath the window, was stiff with horror. The knot of fear in his belly had swollen till it felt as if it filled his whole body.

They can smell me!

The Fierce Dogs hadn't spotted him but they knew he was here anyway; they'd picked out his scent from the other dogs and matched it to that of his litter-sister. These terrifying hounds must have stronger noses than any dog Lucky had ever known. How was he supposed to rescue his friends now?

CHAPTER NINETEEN

The big house was raised further off the ground than the low dog-houses that surrounded it, and a flight of wooden steps led up to the main door. They were the best cover Lucky could hope for just now, and he crouched beneath them, ears pricked for the first hint that he'd been discovered. He'd taken care to roll in some mess that he'd found in the grass – at least now he would smell of the Fierce Dogs. He hoped the deception would be enough.

He wondered what chance he'd have if they did detect him. He certainly couldn't outfight them, or even stare them into a stalemate. Could he hope to outrun them? Sweet could, if she were here. Despair gnawed at his guts. *I'd be caught and torn to pieces before I was halfway across the grass.*

He'd waited for hours now, as the sky darkened and the air cooled and the moon rose, and still he didn't see what he was going to do. He knew his friends had been fed a little; he'd heard the Fierce Dogs carry in bowls of food and drop them clattering to the floor, dry nuggets spilling and rolling. He knew, too, that they were held captive in a tiny room, with a guard at all times – and he knew it was small because he'd heard Daisy's muted whine of complaint. If Daisy thought it was cramped, he dreaded to think how Bella was feeling. He had to do something soon, but his head seemed – for the first time in his life – completely empty. He had no ideas, no ways out. No crafty tricks. It was as if he'd never been a Lone Dog in control of his own destiny.

But I was a Lone Dog, he told himself. *And I was the best.*

He felt as if the Forest-Dog was whispering in his ear, steeling his dog-spirit. Yes, he'd need cunning and stealth, and those were the gifts of the Forest-Dog. Breathing quietly, Lucky shut his eyes and begged.

The Fierce Dogs hadn't spoken much to their prisoners – only to order them about – but they did talk to each other when they prowled outside the house or stood sentry in the deepening darkness. Their actions were precise and controlled, and they seemed to anticipate one another's movements. They were frighteningly disciplined, and they never relaxed their vigilance for a moment. These must have been the prized Fierce Dogs of their disappeared longpaws. Lucky shuddered, remembering with dread his few previous encounters with dogs like these. The only sensible thing to do, ever, was run ...

But Bella, Daisy and Alfie didn't have that option. So Lucky wouldn't run either. In the shadow of the steps, barely daring to breathe, he lay and listened.

Three of the Fierce Dogs came out of the big house. Lucky shrank back, hoping they wouldn't see him, but they didn't come down the steps. They sat above him, unseen, talking in loud sneering voices about their captives.

"We should kill them, Blade," grumbled one of the three, staring out at the huge moon. They were so close; Lucky struggled to keep his breathing silent and his heart steady in his ribs.

"Dagger's right," growled the second. "We should leave their bodies by the fence, so no one else will dare trespass. And besides, they're too much trouble."

"And they eat," added Dagger. "A *lot*. They're as

greedy as if every meal could be their last. A waste of rations is what they are. Pathetic mutts."

"Or we could give them a beating and send them on their way," said the other, with less enthusiasm. "It would be another kind of warning. They'd be sure to spread the word."

"They're not going anywhere." The third dog, the one they'd called Blade, growled her opinion. Lucky recognised her silken voice – she was the Alpha. "Not until they tell us how they found us and how they got in. They're all sticking to this story about jumping the fence, but I don't believe it, do you, Mace?"

"Don't worry, Blade. We'll get the truth out of them," said Mace darkly. "They'll be sorry they ever tried to steal from us."

"Indeed," growled Blade smugly. "I imagine it won't take long to persuade the mangy little mutt. And she'll tell us where the fourth dog is, too. I know he's here somewhere – I can scent him."

Beneath them, Lucky shut his eyes, trying to summon the nerve to act. These glossy, terrifying dogs might be ferocious and ruthless, but they weren't the brightest of creatures. If he'd been in Blade's position, he'd have thought of a hole in the fence as soon as Bella told her ridiculous lie, and sent one of their patrols out to check. It would've been sealed and safe by now.

As he'd expected, the guile of the Forest-Dog would be his salvation – if there was any salvation to be had.

Stealthily he crept out from his hiding place under the steps. He could hear the Fierce Dogs muttering above him, secure in the knowledge that their captives weren't going anywhere. One of them rose and stretched – Lucky heard his claws click and scratch on the wood – and he stopped still. But the dog settled again, grunting and sighing.

It was a nerve-shattering task to cross the grass, moving silently between the shadows. Lucky placed each paw carefully, praying to the Forest-Dog that they wouldn't catch a stronger whiff of his scent – not just yet.

He was a little more than halfway to the fence when he stopped, breathing in and out, calming his jangling nerves. Was this far enough? If he went too far, they wouldn't be tempted to come after him; on the other hand, he had no desire to misjudge the distance, and end up in a Fierce Dog's jaws ...

I can do this. Hunching his shoulders, filling his lungs, he gave a wild, deafening bark, and leapt into the air. Spinning, he dropped to all fours, then dashed in a circle, halted, and howled.

The Fierce Dogs got to their feet, staring at him in

the moonlight, but they looked too dumbfounded to move for a moment. At his howl, more Fierce Dogs stuck their heads out of the house. Lucky lifted his head and howled again, the sound cutting through the still night air. "Hey, *stupid!*"

Blade lowered her head, snarling, but she only raised a paw, hesitating. Clearly his behaviour was too frenzied not to raise her suspicions.

"Mad dogs, sad dogs, stupid crazy bad dogs! *Ha!*" Lucky racked his brains for the worst street insults he could remember from his days in the city. "Your mothers had worms! Your fathers were *foxes!*"

"You little –" roared Dagger, but Lucky barked over him, well into his stride by now.

"You were born in spoil-boxes! You taste so bad, the fleas spit you out! Your mothers were tailless! *You hear me, mange-breeders?* Your fathers licked sharpclaw spit!"

They sprang at him, howling with rage. Lucky hesitated only for an instant, his eyes wide as they raced across the grass, drool flying from their jaws. The insults had done their work, and all of them were after him.

Good!

And … bad!

Lucky spun on his hindlegs, and ran as fast as he could.

He raced for the fence, doubled back, spun and dodged – just as a Fierce Dog snapped its teeth close to his tail. They were fast, but Lucky knew that his insults had upset them. They lunged for him angrily, more erratically than a Pack of Fierce Dogs should. This gave Lucky an advantage. An even bigger advantage was his fear of the Fierce Dogs. It made him dodge and duck and fly. Panting, he hurtled along the fence away from the hole Daisy had scratched out. He had to draw them further away. Hopefully, his friends had heard the commotion. *Now, Forest-Dog,* he thought, *please let Bella be smart enough to make a move …*

Lucky slid to a halt on his haunches, tumbled into a quick reverse and bolted between two pursuing Fierce Dogs. They were enraged now, howling with hate. Saliva from snapping jaws whipped across Lucky's face and he ran again, his heart in his throat.

He was running out of moves, and they were getting wise to him. Maybe it was time to make his own escape? If he could just dodge through the bushes, keep ahead of them long enough to reach the hole under the fence –

Oh no!

Lucky bounced off wire he hadn't seen in the dark, shocked enough to slide on to his flank. Sure enough, the fence took a sharp turn here, right in front of him.

As he scrambled to all fours, shaking and gasping for breath, the semicircle of Fierce Dogs hemmed him in.

He blinked and panted, staring wildly at the sleek Fierce Dogs. They were calm and controlled now, muscles bunched as they regained their discipline and formed a moving, snarling trap around him. Slowly, slowly, they stalked forward, stiff-legged, fearsome teeth bared. In the darkness their eyes glinted with hatred.

"Who's clever now, stinking mongrel?" snarled Mace.

Fur bristling, Lucky backed up till he could go no further, the wire of the fence biting painfully into his haunches.

But that was nothing. There would be worse biting in a minute, far worse. These savage dogs were going to rip him to pieces, limb by limb.

CHAPTER TWENTY

"Blade! Blade!"

Blade's elegant head snapped round, and Lucky realised, with a chill in his blood, that although there were several Fierce Dogs waiting to kill him, one seemed to be missing. Despite her fury, Blade must have sent one of them back to check on the prisoners. And now...?

"They're gone, Blade! The prisoners are *gone*."

Blade whipped her attention back to Lucky, her muzzle curling back from her deadly white teeth Unable to help himself, Lucky shrank against the fence, shivering.

"Where are your friends?' the Alpha hissed. "Are they still in the compound?"

Lucky swallowed. He hoped not.

Blade took a menacing pace towards him. "Tell me, street mutt. Where are they hiding? They can't have got out. Not even with one of their miracle-jumps," she sneered.

Lucky managed a hoarse, brave bark. "I don't know.'

"You don't know? Well, let me see. I could tear you into pieces right here, or you could help me round up your miserable little friends."

"Yes," snarled Dagger. "And then we won't hurt you. Not too much, anyway."

"That's right." Blade wore a horrible grin. "It'll be better for all of you if you tell us where they're hiding. You know, don't you? You've been hiding from us since we caught your little *Pack*" – she spat the word with derision – "so you know where they are now. Speak, stupid dog, and you'll live. You *and* your inferior friends. Submit as you should, and we won't kill you. I think that's as fair as I can be, isn't it? You can hardly ask for a better deal."

Mace sniggered at his leader's side.

Lucky stared into Blade's eyes, trying to control the trembling of his limbs. There wasn't a hint of mercy in those dark depths.

This dog was going to kill him no matter what he did. She was going to kill them all, if she got the chance.

At least the others had escaped. Lucky raised his gaze to look beyond Blade and her cohorts, away into the trees beyond the fence. *Thank you, Forest-Dog,* he thought. *You couldn't save us all, but you saved my friends ...*

A distant clatter of wings.

Lucky blinked.

A crow had flapped up from the tangled branches of the wood, and now circled in the sky, cawing.

A crow, in the dark hours of no-sun? He'd seen the bird before. It was the same crow, the crow that he'd seen in the city, calling to him when he needed a kick of courage. There'd been one in the Fierce Dog's garden, too.

These sightings were a message, surely, reminding him of where he'd come from and what he was: a Lone Dog. A Street Dog, cunning and dirty and wise. It was time to start acting like one.

Lucky followed his instincts. He dived straight between Blade's forepaws. She was shocked motionless just for an instant, staring down; then Lucky rolled, snapping his jaws at her soft underbelly. His teeth closed satisfyingly on skin and flesh, and he tasted blood on his tongue as he heard the Alpha's bark of pain and rage. He squirmed out from beneath her, his teeth still tearing free. Then he was past them all, and racing for the fence.

Surprise had won him a snatch of precious time. There was no ducking and dodging now; just a desperate headlong race for the hole. The big dogs were slow to turn, chaotic in their fury; but now they were after him. He could hear their pounding paws, their wild enraged howls. But above that, there was his own desperate ragged breathing.

He burst through bushes, his muscles and chest burning. His legs felt as if they wouldn't carry him any further, but he forced himself on, running till he thought his heart would burst. The hole in the fence was so close, now, so close, and the Fierce Dogs were crashing through the bushes behind him.

Don't stop. Don't stop. I don't want to be Fierce Dog Dinner…

He could almost feel their hot breath on his haunches as he blundered through the last branches and scrabbled for the hole. It wasn't there – *no!*

Lucky pushed on, sensing the jaws of Blade and her Pack right behind him. How could he have missed it? *Had* he missed it? If he'd missed it he was dead –

There! The hole was ahead of him, a dark smear on the earth, smelling of Daisy and Alfie and Bella. Lucky dived, scrambled, kicked with his hindlegs.

For suffocating seconds the hole was dark and horribly endless. Lucky pulled frantically with his forepaws, squeezing himself through the crushing earth. In a miraculous instant, his head was free, breathing the open air. Then the rest of him was free, too, and his tail was thrashing, scattering earth and dirt. Staggering to a trembling halt, he shook himself violently, then bolted away from the horrible Dog-Garden as fast as his shaking legs would take him.

Behind him, the Fierce Dogs crashed against the fence, flinging themselves in mad rage on to the wire. They couldn't have seen the hole, even when they were right by it. He'd outsmarted them after all. Blade and her cronies were the prisoners now – penned in by that high fence. He heard the crash of their bodies as they ran further along the wire, searching furiously for his escape route.

"Pesky Street Dog!" Blade was snarling.

Lucky bolted further up the slope, then halted and stood very still, panting hard and listening for strange, threatening sounds behind the darkness. At this height, the night was still, punctuated only by the song of crickets and the rustle of a faint breeze, and the aggressive hunting sounds of the Fierce Dogs, fainter now.

Where are the others? Have they gone? Lucky looked

around him, sniffed the ground for any trace of Bella, Daisy or Alfie. There was a faint scent of them, but they weren't close by.

They left me, thought Lucky. The others had run for it, leaving him to fend for himself. And that was fine. Finally, they were thinking like sensible dogs, and running as fast and as far as they could. They'd be OK now.

The bark of delight was almost at his ear, and he jumped.

"Bella?"

His litter-sister charged out of the undergrowth, panting with relief. She put her paws on his shoulders, licking his face enthusiastically. A wave of embarrassed happiness surprised him. They'd been upwind of him; that was the only reason he hadn't smelled them. He must have used up all his Forest-Dog blessings escaping from the Fierce Dogs, to have missed them.

"Lucky!" Bella barked. "You made it!"

Suddenly the others were there as well: Alfie, yapping his excitement, and little Daisy capering at his forepaws, trying to dislodge Bella so she could lick his ears too.

"Daisy! Alfie!" He crouched on his forepaws, wagging his tail frantically as they exchanged happy greetings.

"You waited for me!"

"Of course we did!" yipped Daisy, spinning a circle. "How could we leave you, Lucky? You saved us!"

Alfie's stubby tail thrashed the air. "You were wonderful!"

"You risked your life for us! *Again!*" Daisy was beside herself with gratitude.

"Oh Daisy," he sighed, nuzzling her. "How could I desert you after you brought me that mole?"

Bella seemed calmer now, almost subdued, though her tail still wagged as she pressed her face to Lucky's. "I'm sorry, Lucky. I'm so sorry I didn't listen to you."

He blinked at her, sniffing her face, unable to speak.

"You were right. And I should have listened," she told him softly. "I won't make that mistake again."

His heart swelled. "It doesn't matter." He licked her forehead. "Don't worry, Bella. Right now we need to get moving. Listen."

The four dogs stilled, ears pricked to the night. Not far away they could hear the growls and snarls of the frustrated Fierce Dogs, hunting up and down the fence that stopped them from escaping. They weren't all-powerful – and they weren't Free Dogs either. For all their acute sense of smell, they hadn't found the hole yet – and even if they did, it would take some digging to get them through it. But Lucky wasn't taking any more chances.

"It's time to go," he insisted quietly. "Come on."

This time there was no argument from the others. Alfie sped off into the night, finding the track they'd followed from the camp, and Daisy and Bella followed close at his heels.

Lucky paused to glance back at the fence. He knew the desire for vengeance would be burning in Blade's chest. To be outsmarted would be far more than a humiliation for that proud dog: it would be a challenge.

This wasn't the last they'd hear of her; Lucky was sure of that.

CHAPTER TWENTY-ONE

When he woke, Lucky could make out a pale grey line on the eastern horizon, and their surroundings had taken on colourless but distinct shapes. Thorns and twigs pricked at his hide. The others must have had an uncomfortable no-sun's sleep too, but Lucky had insisted they lie low in the undergrowth until sun-up. If they were tracked down, he didn't want to lead Blade and her Pack to the others back at the camp.

He blinked his eyes clear of the blur of sleep and stretched his stiff and aching muscles, languidly wagging his tail. He padded to the sleeping form of Daisy and nudged her ear.

"Come on, Daisy. Time to move on."

She jerked awake, still nervous after her adventures, and was soon yipping softly at Alfie and pawing him, desperate to get moving. At least, thought Lucky, they finally understood the importance of caution.

"I don't think those Fierce Dogs have found the hole yet," said Lucky quietly, "but we shouldn't hang around. They're bound to try again in daylight."

"Oh yes." Daisy shivered.

Alfie stretched and scratched before trotting on in an eager fashion. The other three followed him, keeping up a brisk pace. The more distance they put between themselves and the Dog-Garden, thought Lucky, the better it would be. They had to leave Blade and her Pack far, far behind them, and the only way to do that was to keep moving.

And, he realised with a heavy heart, it wouldn't even be safe to stay in the camp. He dreaded breaking that news to the others.

Walking was doing his aching body some good, but Lucky still felt sore and tired, and his dark thoughts weren't helping. Bella kept giving him anxious glances, but he wasn't ready to talk.

They came to the long open slope and were in sight of the camp sooner than he expected, but that only reinforced his certainty that they had to leave. They were far too close to danger here.

Mickey bounded to meet them, his intelligent face creased with worry, and Sunshine was at his hindpaws, already barking with relief.

"You're back! Thank goodness! What happened?"

"I'll tell you about it when we're all together, Sunshine." Lucky licked her nose and butted her back in the direction of camp. He tried not to notice how Mickey was looking at him, the anxiety etched on his face.

The Leashed Dogs quickly gathered around, gently placing their longpaw things on the earth before them. When they heard what had happened – mostly in breathless snippets from Alfie and Daisy – they were simply glad to have their friends back. No one was disappointed at their failure to bring back food.

"I can't believe you got away from them." Martha shuddered. "They sound dreadful. And frightening."

"They were *very* frightening," declared Daisy emphatically.

"You should have seen Lucky run!" yipped Alfie. "I thought he was done for, but he got the better of them!"

"He was so brave!" Daisy panted, gazing adoringly at Lucky.

"Will they track us back here?" asked Sunshine.

"No," said Lucky, and took a deep breath. "They

will track our scents to this camp. But they won't find us here, because we're moving on."

For a moment all the dogs were stunned into silence, tails and ears drooping.

"No!" wailed Sunshine. *"Already?"*

"Come on, Sunshine." Martha licked her affectionately, almost knocking the little dog sideways. "I know it's perfect here, but we'll find somewhere else that's just as good."

"Not easily," said Mickey bleakly. "But I do see what Lucky means."

"We're leaving." Bella's tone was brisk. "Unless you want to stay here and wait for Blade and her friends. And let me tell all of you, you do *not* want to wait for Blade."

"No," agreed Alfie with a shiver. "I'm sorry, Sunshine."

Sunshine gave a last mournful whimper, glancing back at the glade with its shade and fresh water. "All right."

"Let's just get going," Bella broke in. "Pick up your longpaw things."

Lucky sighed in frustration but decided not to make any comment. *Let them bring their things if it makes them feel better,* he thought. At least they were moving swiftly to organise themselves, and they'd all accepted they had to abandon this camp. That was a start.

As they headed out of the camp, first along a barren ridge and then down into a gully, Lucky saw the little Pack was doing well in other ways, too. They were barely recognisable as the nervous, inexperienced Leashed Dogs he'd led out of the city.

They no longer smelled of soap and longpaws, but of river-water and trees, of earth and each other. It was a proper, wild smell. They were far scruffier too; even Sunshine no longer looked as if she'd ever suffered careful grooming from a longpaw. To Lucky, the little dog looked much happier trotting along with tangled fur and muddy paws. She and Mickey seemed to be getting along well, and when Mickey suggested they hunt together while they walked, she agreed with enthusiasm.

"Don't go too far!" Lucky warned them.

"Of course not," agreed Mickey seriously. "We'll keep as close to the Pack as we can."

The Pack, thought Lucky as he watched the unlikely hunting pair set off into the bushes that lined the gully. Yes, it *was* nearly a proper Pack. There were hardly any complaints any more, no one stopping to whine about thorns in their fur or bruises on their paw pads. They moved as a unit, watching out for each other without even realising they were doing it.

Dog-spirits coming alive, he thought proudly.

Even Bella was listening to the spirit within her, though she may not admit it or know it. They were learning how to be Free Dogs.

Lucky moved more cautiously as they reached the brow of the next low hill, slinking as low as he could to the ground and flattening his ears. Both Mickey and Bella noticed, and came close to him, one on each flank.

"What's wrong, Lucky?" asked Bella nervously.

"That field down there. It's where we saw those yellow longpaws. Let's be careful."

All the dogs eyed the land below nervously. *Good,* thought Lucky; *they're starting to think before they bark.* From up here he could see more of the field's surroundings: smoke rising from a huge longpaw tower; sluggish streams of yellow-grey water flecked with sickly curdled foam. Even the roads beside the field were stained with grimy suds where the water and foam had leaked, perhaps from that tower. Lucky shuddered, then shook himself. He was glad they'd got away from that terrible place while they could. It made him think of panic, and sickness, and death.

He picked up speed a little as they left. It was good to put these things behind them, and Lucky had started to relax, to feel free and easy once more as he listened happily to the chatter of Sunshine and Daisy behind him.

Then he heard a longpaw bark.

Lucky froze, one paw in mid-air. A ripple of fear went down his spine. The others, of course, pricked their ears and one or two gave yelps of excitement, but it was Bella who snapped at them.

"Calm down!" Bella growled. "Be quiet! Have you forgotten what happened to Daisy!"

"Oh yes," whispered Daisy. "Let's be very careful."

Placing one paw cautiously in front of the other, Lucky crept through the trees and bushes ahead. There was a low building there, visible beyond its rusty wire fence, that reminded him of the Fierce Dogs' home. Even though they were far away from Blade and Dagger and the rest, Lucky didn't like it at all. Nervously he crouched and sniffed at the fence.

A crash of branches ahead and to one side almost made him yelp out loud; but instead he went as still as he could, cringing against a tree trunk and hoping he wouldn't be seen. The longpaw – the one who'd barked, he was sure – had burst from the thick bushes, but his shape seemed strange: bulky and uneven. Lucky realised instantly why – there was a dead deer slung over the longpaw's shoulder. In the longpaw's other hand was a loudstick – and one that had recently spat fire and death, judging by the acrid, pungent smell. But there was another smell too: the smell of fresh blood, wafting from the deer carcass. Prey. *Food ...*

Lucky was slinking backwards into the trees as the longpaw hauled a door open in the low building, and began to carry the deer inside. He wouldn't have noticed the dogs at all, if the Pack had managed to stay quiet.

But then Bruno dashed forward, barking a greeting, and Mickey, Sunshine and Alfie could no longer contain themselves either. Bella growled at them to come back, but only Daisy and Martha remained subdued, the littlest dog huddled and trembling beneath her friend's legs. The rest were yelping their joy at the longpaw, running towards it, ears flying.

He spun round, dropping the deer in a thudding heap, and his eyes widened.

The longpaw gave another furious bark, and brought the loudstick to its shoulder, pointing it at the running dogs.

Lucky trembled as terror lifted his fur. Didn't the others *know* about loudsticks? Didn't they know what those terrible things could do? He was about to bark a warning when the loudstick exploded.

The sound was a crack as loud as the Big Growl. It echoed in the clearing, ringing in Lucky's ears, and it brought the running dogs to a terrified, skidding halt.

Lucky skittered forward, nervous, but worried for his friends. He saw instantly that none of them were hurt; the loudstick must have been pointing over their heads when it exploded.

While they were cowering back, the longpaw turned and dragged the deer inside the building, then slammed the door with a thundering clang.

The four dogs gathered their wits – but Lucky could barely believe what he was seeing. Instead of turning tail and running for their lives, they were bounding towards the low building again.

Bruno flung his stocky body at the door with a crash, and immediately the others were scratching at it too, whining and yelping and whimpering. Stopping only to exchange one disbelieving look with Bella, Lucky raced forward, his litter-sister at his heels.

"Come away, you fools! What on earth are you doing?"

"Bruno!" barked Bella. "Didn't you see the loudstick? Didn't you *hear*?"

Bruno shook her off, and scratched at the door again. "It's only a *gun*, Bella! My longpaw had a gun! He hunted deer, just like that one!"

"And don't you see, Bella?" cried Mickey. "He didn't

shoot us! And he wasn't a *bad* longpaw. He wasn't one of the eyeless ones with the yellow fur."

"Oh," yelped Alfie. "Oh Bella! The longpaw has a whole deer in there! If he lets us in, he'll share it. He can't eat a *whole deer!* We can help him!" Alfie yapped wildly at the door again.

A volley of angry longpaw barks from within made Lucky twitch.

Sunshine looked a little less certain than the others, and cast nervous looks back at Martha and the shivering Daisy. "Maybe Bella's right, Mickey. The longpaw did try to scare us, even if it didn't … hurt us …"

"He'll kill you next time," snarled Lucky furiously. "He already gave you a warning with his loudstick …"

"Thank you, Lucky!" Bella interrupted. She waited for the look of surprise to fade from his face. "You're right, of course." She turned to the rest of the dogs. "I miss my longpaws as much as you all do, but *this* one isn't our longpaw. We can't chase after every longpaw we see!"

For the first time, Bruno, Mickey and Alfie looked uncertain. "But Bella …" whimpered Alfie.

"It's no good," scolded Bella firmly. "You *have* to stop and think. Hasn't Lucky got through to you at *all?*"

The others looked downright ashamed now. Lucky

looked up at his litter-sister, pride and nervousness jangling together in his mind. He was truly impressed with Bella's leadership. The four runaways were certainly submitting to her, lowering their heads, tucking their tails between their hindlegs, creeping back to their friends in the trees. Bella was going to make a good Alpha for this group.

They would not need to depend on Lucky any more.

Daisy yipped softly with relief at their return. "Come on, Mickey," she begged. "Let's leave that longpaw here with his prey. That's all he's thinking of just now. Let's go on, quickly!"

"You're right, Daisy." Mickey sounded ashamed of himself. "I'm sorry. We're all sorry, Bella." He licked her nose apologetically. "We didn't think."

"It's all right," said Bella. "But from now on, we all have to be wary of longpaws. We don't *know* them. They aren't ours, and you must all remember that."

As they headed on up the valley, quieter now, Lucky padded at Bella's side. When he licked her jaw, she gave him a quizzical glance, but looked happy.

She's starting to understand, thought Lucky, with a warm sense of relief and pride.

They moved quickly after that, unnerved by their encounter with the longpaw. Breaks to rest, or to drink and eat, were brief, though Lucky took plenty of time to praise Sunshine in particular when she and Mickey returned from their foray with a rabbit. They needed encouragement now, after their shock and their fierce scolding from Bella.

But still, they were all coping much better than before. Even when they'd travelled over more land than he'd ever covered and the Sun-Dog was setting across the western hills, there were few complaints. It was Lucky, recognising that Sunshine and Daisy were almost at the end of their endurance, who barked encouragement from the ridge of a hill.

"We're stopping to rest here. Look!"

All of them came right up beside him before flopping down, heads on paws, to gaze at the view.

"Oh my," breathed Martha.

"Is that our *city?*" gasped Sunshine.

From their vantage point, they could see more than even Lucky ever had before. The shoreline was a curved ribbon of silver and the ocean an expanse of blue that stretched to a brilliant horizon. The precipitous hill at their paws sloped down to fields and broad plains of grass, and further on, neatly groomed squares of green, made tiny by distance.

And there, too, was their city. Lucky stared. Even

more from this angle than up close in its streets, Lucky could see the changes in one great sprawling vista. There were gaps, like patches of skin in mangy fur, where buildings had simply ceased to exist, and lakes of silver water shimmered where there should be none. Great rivers of poisoned grey-yellow water, ran between the ruined buildings.

No one had spoken since Bella's outburst. Now, she stepped forward to face her friends.

"Listen to me," she said. "This is a different world." Bella gave Lucky a sidelong glance, and he nodded, giving her a soft woof of encouragement.

Bella addressed her Pack again, more confidently. "You can see almost the whole of it from here, can't you? The whole world. You can see how it's changed. And a different world," Bella took a moment to gaze into each Pack member's eyes, "needs a different kind of dog."

Daisy whimpered uneasily. Solemnly, Martha returned Bella's gaze. "You're not just telling us the world has changed, Bella. Are you?"

Bella took a breath, but the only nerves she showed were in the anxious thumping of her tail. "We have to survive on our own. We have to learn – we don't have a choice."

"But Bella," whined Alfie, "we're trying. We

really are."

"I know! We're acting like a real Pack! But we'll never truly be self-reliant if we don't trust ourselves." Bella pawed Alfie's longpaw ball where he'd let it drop. "We need to accept that we're alone, and we need to rely on ourselves, and no one else. Not even our longpaws. We're going to," Bella took a deep breath, "we're going to leave these things of theirs behind."

Mickey dropped his glove in shock, and stared at it, then at Bella. "Leave them? Bella, we can't!"

"We have to! Don't you see? Until we leave these things in the past where they belong, we'll never truly trust ourselves, or each other. We need to accept these are our old lives! For now, Mickey, at least. They were important, but they are *past*. Please believe me." Bella's ears drooped, and she added quietly, "Maybe Lucky's right. Maybe we need to try harder to listen to our dog-spirits."

Lucky had never felt prouder of anything in his life.

Mickey gazed mournfully at Bruno, who lay down with a great sigh, his bulky head on his paws. But Alfie broke the miserable silence with an angry bark.

"But Lucky doesn't understand. And I'm starting to think you don't, either, Bella!"

"Alfie's right," said Mickey, rising on to all fours.

"I know it doesn't make sense to Lucky, but Bella, you know how much this matters!"

What matters, Lucky wanted to yelp in frustration, *is that you give these things up!* But he knew how important it was, especially for Bella, that he kept quiet, so he said nothing.

"It matters," said Bella quietly, "but our survival matters more."

"You're only saying that because Lucky thinks it!" yelped Alfie. "You're just trying to please your brother!"

"That's nonsense!" snapped Bella. "I'm saying it because it's true."

"No, Bella!" squealed Sunshine, planting a paw on her yellow leash. "No, I won't throw this away! My longpaw bought it for me and it's *special!*"

"That's right!" grunted Bruno, taking the peaked cap back into his mouth as if Bella was going to snatch it away.

Alfie's eyes were alight with anger. "I'm surprised at you, Bella. We won't abandon our longpaws!"

"Then none of us will survive!" she barked. "We'll always be looking over our shoulders for help from our longpaws. And I know it now, and so do you if you're honest: *they aren't coming back!*"

As each of the dogs began snapping and yelping

with indignation, Daisy sat suddenly back and gave a howl of misery.

The others looked at her, shocked, and then at each other.

"Please don't fight!" she whimpered. "I hate it when we fight!"

Bella turned to the small dog and licked her head reassuringly. "I'm sorry. You're right. It doesn't do any good to squabble." Determinedly she lifted her head to gaze once more at the others.

Lucky hardly dared to breathe as he watched the scene unfold. He couldn't interrupt. Not when so much hung in the balance. They'd already learned from their Fierce Dog escape that it was worth listening to Lucky – and now to Bella. Would that lesson be remembered?

Martha was the first to move. After a few long moments she bent down and picked up her red scarf. His heart in his throat, Lucky thought she was going to defy Bella, turn and walk away into an uncertain, dangerous future.

Instead, she found a patch of soft earth and began to scrape at it with her forepaws. With her huge webbed paws it didn't take long to dig a small hole. The rest watched, silent, as the soil flew. When the hole was perhaps a foreleg deep, she lifted her scarf, and dropped it gently into the ground.

The other dogs shared anxious glances. A little grumpily, Bruno followed suit with his cap, Alfie with his ball, and Sunshine with her glittering lead. Her expression was tragic as she slowly covered the sparkling stones with layers of soil. Daisy took longer to dig a deep enough hiding place for her battered leather pouch, but Martha helped her, and soon they had both pawed earth back over their longpaw things. Lucky watched them in silence, afraid to break the spell of their dog-spirits; surely now they were listening to those inner voices. Finally Bella picked up her own grubby bear-toy, and buried it in the earth.

Only when she was done she glanced at Mickey, the last one left. Mickey placed a paw on his glove. "This was my longpaw pup's most precious possession, Bella. I know how much it mattered to him. He wouldn't have left it if he could help it. And I know for certain he wouldn't have left me either."

Bella gazed at him, thoughtful. The other dogs looked from one to the other.

Fondly Mickey nuzzled the glove's worn leather, then raised his head. "I can't give up my faith in the longpaws. I don't think you have, either. I understand why we have to leave these things – truly, Bella, I do. I understand we can't rely on the longpaws to help us any more. But one of us has to remember. One of us has to carry the memories for the rest of the Pack." He lifted the glove delicately in his jaws. "I'll do it."

Bella gave a soft accepting bark. "Perhaps you're right, Mickey. And we can all help you carry it sometimes – that means we'll all have a part in looking after the memory." She nuzzled Mickey's face fondly.

Giving them a last brief time with their longpaw things, Lucky padded a little way down the hill and looked back. Each of the dogs stood over their mound of disturbed earth, howling at the sky. The sight and the sound gave Lucky a pang of mixed emotion. They were mourning their longpaws, certainly – but they were sending their cries out into the world! Whether they knew it or not, they were also making peace with the Earth-Dog.

As Bella's voice raised above the howls of the others, he felt his heart swell in his ribcage with love and pride.

"Earth-Dog!" cried his litter-sister. "Earth-Dog, keep our things safe!"

"And us, too!" howled Mickey. "Earth-Dog: bring the longpaws home to us, too."

Lucky couldn't share their sorrow, but he did feel an aching fondness for them all. His heart was sore with affection and sympathy, but at the same time he was light-headed with gladness that it wasn't like this for him.

He was free and easy Lucky.

A Lone Dog.

CHAPTER TWENTY-TWO

It was late the following day, after a long and tiring plod through forest and stream, when Lucky found the valley. Because of the sweeping angle of its slopes, it wasn't visible till his forepaws were on the edge of the steep ridge above it.

As the others padded up to his side, weary, their fur thick with the dust of travel, Lucky gazed out silently at the scene before him. A clear river flowed through the centre of the valley, diverted by rocks and hillocks and clusters of trees and bushes, but apart from those places of shade and shelter, the space was broad and open. A Pack of dogs in this valley would be able to see trouble coming from a long way off. And there were no huge trees or high rock faces to tumble and fall and trap them, should the earth Growl again …

It was perfect. His friends would be safe here. He wouldn't have to feel guilty about leaving them, moving on, being a loner again.

He should feel happy about that – so why this twist of sadness in his belly?

At his flank, Daisy gave a whine, but it was a whine of hope, not complaint. The low, late Sun-Dog gilded the grasslands below and turned the river gold.

"Lucky! Do you think – could we –"

"I think you just might, Daisy," he told her softly.

"*We* might, you mean?" she yapped, confused.

He didn't have to answer, because Bruno was harrumphing happily at the view now. "This is great! Lucky, you genius!"

"It's beautiful," breathed Alfie. "Wonderful!"

"And there'll be plenty to hunt," Lucky pointed out as Bella and Mickey joined them. "That's ideal territory for mice and rabbits."

Bruno was shifting from forepaw to forepaw. "Lucky! Does this mean the Earth-Dog liked our offerings?"

Lucky was perplexed only for an instant. "Your longpaw possessions? Well, maybe …"

"I think Bruno's right!" yapped Alfie. "The Earth-

Dog is pleased with us at last, and she's brought us here!"

Lucky agreed that it was a piece of good luck. "It's a perfect place. You'll be happy here, and you'll hunt and eat well. But best of all, you'll be as safe as you can possibly be." He licked Alfie's nose, feeling a little pang of fondness for him. "I'm glad."

"But –" Alfie was dumbfounded.

Bruno broke in. "You can't mean you're going?"

Lucky averted his eyes, and kept his bark cheerful. "Of course I am. That was always the plan!"

The chorus of dismayed howls that greeted his announcement rocked him back on his hindlegs.

"You can't leave us alone!" cried Sunshine.

Lucky licked the top of her head. "I'm a Lone Dog. I have to be on my own."

"But you're part of our Pack!" whined Daisy.

"No! You don't need me! Look at how well you've been hunting. You can take care of yourselves, and you're listening to your dog-spirits – that's the most important thing. You're a team, a proper Pack, and now you have a perfect place to live!"

"Oh, Lucky." Bella padded forward, licked his nose, and sat down squarely in front of him, gazing into his eyes as her tail slowly thumped the earth.

Lucky felt his heart sink. *Please*, he thought. *Please*,

Bella, don't try to stop me. I can't bear to fight with you, not after everything we've been through just to survive …

"Don't worry." She touched her nose to his. "I won't argue with you again. But I'm going to ask you one thing. Stay one more no-sun with us."

"Oh, *yes!*" barked Sunshine. "Lucky, do!"

"Oh, please!" Daisy's expression was pleading, and the others were barking enthusiastically in agreement.

"Just one more no-sun." Bella's gaze wouldn't let him go. "If you feel the same at sun-up, we won't try to stop you. Even *I* won't argue." She cocked one ear and tilted her head. "That's fair, isn't it?"

Lucky sighed and closed his eyes. He wouldn't change his mind and he knew it; he'd always felt this way, and it was how he'd still feel at sun-up.

But could it really hurt? One more night sleeping curled up with his friends, feeling the warmth and companionship he hadn't known since the Pup-Pack. One more night of comfort, and then, at sun-up, his old life back: freedom and the wilderness, a solitary happiness. It was what he wanted, what he always longed for, and if there was a tiny voice inside him crying like a pup to stay with his friends, then it was only an ancient memory; an almost-dead instinct from a blurred time he could barely remember.

"Yes," he said at last. "All right. But I warn you, I won't change my mind."

***

Lucky lay, head on his paws, and watched in startled awe as the dogs of his temporary Pack worked around him, an efficient team under the confident direction of Bella. *They've come so far,* he thought with a twinge of affection.

Alfie and Sunshine had been sent to fetch mouthfuls of long dry grass from the valley, which they had strewn across a long boulder by the river. They sat panting now, admiring their hard work. On top of the grass the others had carefully placed the results of their last hunting trip – which Lucky had not been allowed to join.

"You're our guest!" Daisy had yapped.

"So that we can say farewell," added Bella quietly.

It had been entirely different when he was staying out of the hunt to let them learn. Now Lucky felt very awkward not helping, but Bruno had given him an amiable snap of his teeth every time he'd offered.

"Lie down and wait in peace, Lucky!"

So Lucky did. He had to admit, once he'd relaxed, it had been a nice sun-high lying in the dappled shadows by the new river, listening to the flow of the water. Now they had all returned – Mickey trotting back last, a limp and bloody rabbit in his jaws – and one by one they placed their prey on the bed of grass.

Shyly, Daisy laid down a rather crumpled mouse. Bella had caught another rabbit, and Martha had somehow managed to catch a squirrel. Bruno and Mickey between them had made the star catch: a small deer that they'd surprised and trapped. It lay in a place of pride in the centre of the spread. Alfie and Sunshine had even brought back some beetles as well as their haul of grass.

There was a lump in Lucky's throat as they formed a semicircle around him and the food. Bella stalked forward and lowered herself on to her forelegs, then bowed her head.

"We've caught this prey for you, Lucky. For all you've done for us. Please will you eat first?"

Lucky swallowed. He'd never seen anything like this, and he was embarrassed, but touched. Out of their own habits and rituals with their longpaws, they'd created this ceremony especially for him. He was grateful for the thought they'd put into their last meal together.

"Go on, Lucky." Sunshine pricked her white ears hopefully. "Take the first bite of everything!"

Obediently he paced up to the strewn prey, and took a beetle delicately between his teeth, then crunched and gulped it down. Sunshine looked ridiculously pleased that he'd chosen her offering first, and her fluffy tail thudded the earth with delight.

Lucky took great care to tear small pieces from every single offering, chewing even as he whined his appreciation. Only when he'd tasted everything did they all come forward and join in. Soon they were all happily wolfing down chunks of rabbit and deer and squirrel.

"You're hunters," he said, pausing to swallow and gaze around at them. "You have a real talent for finding food. Thank you for this."

"Thank *you*, Lucky," murmured Martha. "It's you who made us hunters."

When they lay down at last in a contented huddle, their bellies full, Lucky closed his eyes with a long sigh. Bella once again lay against him; Daisy had flopped over his haunches, while Sunshine was tucked under his throat. Mickey's hindlegs were tucked cosily under Lucky's flank, and as he drifted into sleep he felt them twitch; *Ah*, he thought with amusement, *so Mickey's dreaming of chasing that deer …*

***

Darkness. Again. But so different this time!

Lucky couldn't sense the wire of the Trap House. There was nothing hemming him in but this black emptiness … and the snarling, tumbling, thrashing bodies of dogs.

Dogs fighting each other! Fighting to the death, in a storm – the Storm of Dogs.

Turning, spinning desperately, he could see no way out. Claws raked at his flank, fangs flashed as they snapped. A huge dog crashed against him, then was gone, tearing back into the battle. The noise was dreadful: howling, screaming, snapping. All around him was fury and pain and terror. Wildly flailing fangs caught his ear and tore it; the pain seemed to pierce his skull.

It was like the final battle of the Sky-Dogs, the one his mother had told him would come one day. Yes! That was it, it had to be – the war at the world's end. And he was in the middle of it, cowering and ducking from the savagery of the warriors.

There were other dogs he knew – Bella, there close to his side, screaming as a huge red-eyed hound bowled her over on to her back and lunged for her throat. NO, he thought, NO – but he couldn't reach her. Paws and claws were pulling him down. There was Sweet, too, crippled and dying, unable to run. And Blade and Dagger, snapping, tearing, biting, but then they too were overwhelmed by the dark mass of dogs. Little Daisy vanished, howling, beneath the crash of bodies. And there was nothing he could do. Nothing!

He tried to lunge for Daisy's collar, but his paws slipped helplessly in water ... no. Not water. It was warm, slippery, dark ... blood that rose steadily, lapping around his paws, clinging to his fur. The surface of it was sheened with something evil: a slick of poison like the one on the bad river. Terrified, he staggered, and slipped, and fell. Now his mouth was full of blood, the metallic tang of it. His teeth were coated in it, sticky and vile. And his eyes – they were filling with it too, and all he could see was red.

Blood red ...

Lucky sprang to his feet, trembling from head to tail, gasping for breath. His heart thrashed inside his ribcage as if it would burst right through. The sky and the whole world was blood red, and for horrible moments he could still taste dog blood in his mouth.

Then he realised: it was the dawn. The Sun-Dog was yawning, and stretching, and making the sky glow scarlet as he rose.

Lucky still couldn't control the beating of his heart, and he couldn't repress a terrified whimper. Beside him, Daisy stirred and stretched questioningly, half-rising to lick at his muzzle.

"Lucky? Are you all right?"

He glanced down, shocked, as a wave of relief buffeted him. Daisy wasn't dead, then, crushed and torn beneath the weight of battling dogs; she was here with him, and safe. He licked her nose in return, swamped by gratitude.

"I'm OK, Daisy. It was … a bad dream. That's all."

She didn't have to know the details, he decided. He'd keep those to himself – even though the horror of the dream still clung to him, and fear shivered in his cold hide.

The others were stirring now, stretching in the warmth of the Sun-Dog, licking one another in greeting, yawning. As they stood up, shaking off sleep, they seemed to remember very suddenly, and as one, what the dawn meant for them and for Lucky. Their sun-up yelps and growls quieting, they all turned sadly towards him. Martha padded close and nuzzled his face.

"Lucky," she whined softly, "what will we do without you?"

Firmly ignoring his own ache of regret, Lucky yapped with determined eagerness.

"You'll be fine! I have to look after myself. I'm sure you don't want to be responsible for me."

"I wouldn't mind that," whimpered Daisy mournfully.

"But, Daisy!" Lucky wagged his tail energetically, hating their distress and forcing lightness into his bark. "You're growing up so fast. You're a strong hunting dog, and you're going to be even stronger. Next time I see you, you'll be showing off, bringing me rabbits two at a time! And I will see you again, I promise. I'll come back to visit."

Daisy dipped her head and woofed sadly. "Oh, Lucky. I'll miss you so much."

"And I'll miss you," he told her fondly. "But just think, you won't have me nagging and bullying you!" He jumped up, thrashing his tail and bouncing in a circle, barking enthusiastically. "Aren't you going to say goodbye properly?"

They fell on him, barking and licking and nuzzling their farewells. Lucky licked and woofed and whined in return, crushing down the pang of regret in his heart and gut. He would not change his mind, so why feel any remorse? They'd be fine without him, and he'd be happy alone.

"Bruno, goodbye. Stay brave, stay strong. Martha, there's a river. You'll be able to swim again! Daisy, Sunshine, Alfie – I think you're twice your size, inside.

Just you listen to your dog-spirits, because I think they're fiercer than any Fierce Dogs!" He turned to Mickey, accepting his solemn goodbye licks. "Mickey, you're a great hunter. Teach them well! And you, Bella –"

He quietened as his litter-sister padded up and pressed her face to his.

"Ah, Lucky," she murmured. "Do we have to lose each other again?"

"Oh, Bella." He felt a stab of hurt in his belly. "At least we can say goodbye properly this time, not like when the longpaws took us from the Pup-Pack."

"That changed you forever," she said softly.

"Yes." He sighed. "I'm not sorry, Bella. I'm glad my life has been like this. But I wouldn't have left you, you know. If we hadn't been parted by longpaws."

"I know." She licked his ear. "I know you're not like us. You're a different kind of dog, and you love what you are. That's good, Lucky. And you've helped us. So much. Thank you for staying with us all this time."

"No ... thank *you* for being my friends. I'm so glad to have travelled with you." He was shocked by how true it was, by the sharp pain of loss he felt at leaving them.

"Goodbye, Lucky. But only for now." Bella gave him a last affectionate nuzzle, then took a pace back.

Lucky spun on his haunches and howled with

happiness, drowning the ache of remorse that threatened to close his throat. "I'll see you again! Be happy! *Good luck!* I'll miss you."

Before he could change his mind, he bounded away, back down the hill, leaving the beautiful valley they'd found for a home. Racing fast, as if he could outpace the memories, he dodged trees and leapt fallen trunks, revelling in his re-found freedom.

After all, the goodbye *wasn't* forever. He'd seen right to the ocean from that vantage point where he'd left his friends, and as far as the mountains to the other side. The world wasn't nearly as big as he'd thought. Eventually, he knew, his journey would bring him back to them. And how much they'd have to tell one another, of hunts and adventures and fun …

The Sun-Dog's rays dappled the forest floor in patches of green and gold, and the birds were singing unseen in the branches. Ahead of him he saw a crow perched, watching him, till it took off with a great flap of black wings, cawing what sounded like a greeting to a friend. The air smelled fresh and alive, full of growth and energy. He loved the forest; he always had! That was why the Forest-Dog had come to his rescue at the Fierce Dog-place, with his gift of guile and cunning. Now he would be close to the Forest-Dog again. He would be solitary, free and happy; hunting and living for himself alone. Just as he'd always loved to live.

A squirrel darted across his path, startled by his sudden bounding appearance and scurrying in a panic for the nearest tree. Lucky barked happily and made a half-hearted dash for it, not yet hungry enough to care if he caught it. As it fled into the topmost branches, turning to chatter angrily at him, he panted and barked with pure delight, spinning on his hindlegs.

"Next time!" he yelped cheerfully. "Next time, squirrel!"

And then he froze, his tongue still hanging stupidly out. What was that sound?

One paw raised, he turned, uncertain.

There were frenzied howls and barks behind him, but it wasn't the unearthly, blood-chilling screaming of his dreams. So what ...?

Dogfight!

Back there, in the distance, where he'd come from. Where the others were. He'd left them, thinking they were safe. An enraged violent barking rose above the rest, and Lucky cocked his ears to listen, his bones thrilling with fear. It wasn't the Fierce Dogs, and it wasn't his friends –

"Our territory! This is our place! OURS!"

Lucky glanced at the crow in the branches ahead,

as it watched him. He gazed around at the green-and-golden forest, so full of life, such a perfect place for a Lone Dog.

Then he turned, and sprang back the way he'd come, racing through the trees. Jumping, dodging, leaping fallen branches; but always, always heading back to where he'd left his friends. They were in danger. They needed him. He had to go to them. *Now!*

He was conscious of only one thing as his muzzle drew back, baring his fangs for a fight …

They were *his* Pack.

Lucky's Pack …

And they were in trouble.

To be continued …

DON'T MISS THE SECOND THRILLING ADVENTURE ...

The Leashed Dogs have settled in the forest, but a menacing Pack of Wild Dogs threatens to drive them away. Lucky must go behind enemy lines on a mission that will put his loyalties to the test. The lines between the Packs blur and not every dog will survive!

ISBN: 9781787004498

'Perfectly crafted.'

KIRKUS REVIEWS (STARRED REVIEW)

HUBERT HORATIO

How to Raise your Grown-UPS

First published
in Great Britain
by
HarperCollins *Children's Books* in 2018
Published in this edition in 2019
HarperCollins *Children's Books* is a division of HarperCollins*Publishers* Ltd,
HarperCollins Publishers
1 London Bridge Street
London SE1 9GF

The HarperCollins website address is
www.harpercollins.co.uk

1

ISBN 978–0–00–826409–3

Original text design by David Mackintosh
Printed and bound in England by CPI Group (UK) Ltd, Croydon CR0 4YY

MIX
Paper from
responsible sources
FSC™ C007454